Emma and the Reindeer

EMMA AND THE REINDEER

Emma Gallagher

First published in the United States by Restart Communications, LLC, Indianapolis, Indiana, USA.

EMMA AND THE REINDEER

LindaMansfieldBooks.com

EmmaAndTheReindeer.com

EmmaAndTheReindeer@gmail.com

ISBN (EPUB): 978-0-9968617-8-6

ISBN (Paperback): 978-0-9968617-7-9

ISBN (Hardcover): 978-0-9968617-6-2

ISNB (Audiobook): 978-0-9968617-9-3

Library of Congress Control Number: 2025901037

Contents

Dedication

In memory of Robert N. Strauss

Quintessential New Yorker
Horseplayer extraordinaire
Veteran
Letters-to-the-editor writer
Best copy editor ever
Terrific boss
Cherished friend

3

Grandma Hazel

I was at the desk in my bedroom and had just decided to do the rest of my homework later when I heard the faint sound of bells outside my window. I stood up to investigate, and out of the corner of my eye I saw something move on my bed. I tried to speak, but not even air came out. The tiniest woman I had ever seen was standing on my mattress.

She couldn't be more than 2 feet tall.

She gripped the bed's footboard with her left hand for balance. She stroked the back of my calico cat with her right hand. Pansy usually hides when a stranger is around, but she was purring and leaning against the woman, who was looking straight at me.

"Hello, Emma. Don't be afraid."

A shiver slid down my spine, but the lump in my throat wouldn't move. I just stood by my desk and stared.

The woman's hair was styled in a bob, parted down the middle. One side of her hair was neon red, and the other side was neon green. The two colors met at her part and in the middle of her forehead because she had bangs. It gave her a very divided look.

She wore an old-fashioned forest-green vest and a cream-colored blouse printed with candy canes. She also wore a long, brown tweed skirt. Her gold taffeta slippers turned up at the toes into little hooks. Small gold tassels dangled from each hook, and beside each tassel was a string of tiny gold bells.

I swept the room with my eyes and then zeroed in on the alarm clock on my nightstand. Its blue neon lights said 7:57 p.m.

How could that be? It was 7:57 when I closed my notebook.

I stepped across the cold hardwood floor toward the bed, dodging some piles of books, board games, and a couple of puzzles. The ceiling light was on, but the March moon splashed additional silver light through the window.

When I got to the bed, I pressed the switch on the lamp on my bedside table to get a better look at the woman. Something spicy, like cinnamon, peppered the air.

The woman moved some of her hair on both sides of her head over her ears, which were bigger than regular ears and pointy at the top.

I rubbed my right eye with my right index finger and shook my head. "Who are you?" came out, followed by "How did you get into my bedroom?"

"I've waited a long time to meet you, Emma," the little woman said, smiling at me. "I'm your Grandma Hazel Gallagher. Fifteenth great-grandma, to be exact."

A great-grandma? What?

Something about her smile and honest tone made me think she might be telling the truth, but how could that be?

If she really was a relative and she had waited a long time to meet me, I guess I should try to be hospitable.

"Would you like a glass of water?" I asked. "Sorry my room is such a mess." Mom had asked me to put some of my stuff away this afternoon, but I told her I'd do it tomorrow.

"No, I'm fine, Emma; thank you," the woman said. Pansy was now in a ball, purring by the woman's feet. The woman tiptoed around the cat, held onto the footboard for support, used my comforter to rappel down to the floor, and turned to continue to talk to me. "Let me get right to the point. I'm here because I have an important job for you to do, should you be willing."

"What is it?"

"Santa and I, and really all of us, were impressed with the book you started writing last summer," she began.

"Nobody knows about that book," I interrupted. "I never finished it. It's a secret. And who? Santa? Nobody believes in Santa Claus."

"Santa knows everything, child," the woman said, undaunted. "The notebooks you used are in a brown box right now, under your bed."

She was right. Creative writing is my favorite class in school, and I've been thinking about trying to become a writer or a journalist when I grow up.

The clock on my nightstand must be broken. It was still the same time it had been earlier — 7:57 p.m.

"Are you an elf? Do you live at the North Pole?" I asked.

"Santa's Workshop, which is a whole kingdom, is always near the North Pole, but the kingdom moves," she said. "We have to take measures to keep our location a secret.

"The North Pole itself is all ice; it constantly floats on top of the Arctic Ocean. We move, not only to keep those snoopy satellites from discovering us, but because sometimes we need to be on land so our animals can graze. Other times the kingdom floats above the surface of the Earth, just beyond the Northern Lights. It's quite remarkable."

I fingered the bottom hem of my sweatshirt. "We talked about those lights in science class," I said. "They're beautiful."

"Yes, they are," she agreed.

I heard a deep breath escape from my mouth. My head tilted slightly to one side as I waited for her to say more.

"Emma, I've come to see if you would be willing to undertake an important assignment that could save both Christmas and the Earth," she said.

Is that all? I thought.

"I'm just a girl. I'm 11 and a half," I cautioned.

"Never say you're 'just' a girl," she said. "Girls are wonderful! But I need to get to the point. We need a boy or girl who can conduct some interviews and write a book to set the record straight on a few things, and convince children to take measures now to save the environment and life on Earth as we know it. It will also save Christmas.

"Santa's reindeer need to eat magic lichen all year in order to fly on Christmas Eve, and with climate change they're having trouble getting enough of it," she explained. "We think we'll have enough this year, but future Christmases are in jeopardy."

It was a lot to think about. I know the environment is in bad shape. I know glaciers are melting, but I never thought that might stop Christmas from happening. But there's not much I can do about it. I'm no Greta Thunberg, after all. Write a book? Well, I tried, but I couldn't finish the one I started.

"Why a book? And why do you want a kid to write it?" I asked.

"At the North Pole, we believe in the power of literature to change the world," she said. "In more practical terms, books are good because you can read them anywhere, and even if children don't have any money they can read books for free from libraries."

Then she frowned. "As for why a kid should write it, it's because the grown-ups haven't done a good job protecting the environment. We're seeing bad changes firsthand because the sea is warming. That causes bad things to happen on land because everything in the environment is interconnected. The Earth's only hope is the next generation, and we feel a member of it would be best to relate the message of sustainability most urgently."

"Oh," was all I said in reply.

"Yes," she continued, unfazed. "And considering that your book is about global warming, we thought you'd be the perfect author, if you'd be willing to do it."

My book *was* about global warming. I blinked. "I don't know if I can write a whole book. That's a lot of pages."

"We're sure you can do it if you try, and you will do a wonderful job," she said. "We'll have Santa read it before you send it to an agent or a publisher to be sure it's correct and no secrets are disclosed. Santa is jolly, but he's also secretive."

"I don't know," I repeated, shaking my head. "I want to be a writer someday, but I'm just a kid. I get A's in English and I love reading, but writing a whole book is very hard."

"We know you can do it if you try," she insisted.

"Why didn't you just call or email me rather than break into our house?"

"This is an important assignment," she said. "I wanted to speak to you about it in person, with no distractions. And people often freak out when they meet an elf, so I must be careful."

"I'm a little freaked out," I admitted.

"You're doing fine, Emma."

She was so, I don't know, positive. But something else was bothering me. "If you're an elf, and you're my great-grandma from a long time ago, then am I an elf too?"

"You have elf blood in you, but you identify as a human," she said. "It all depends on your dominant chromosomes."

She had an answer for everything. "Are my mom and dad or my brother Jacob elves?"

"No, they're all humans, just like you," she answered. "Your mother has the most elf blood in your immediate family, but she's a human."

"And you're really my ancestor?"

"Yes, I'm your Great-Grandma Hazel, 15 times removed," she assured me. "I was married to your Great-Grandpa Thomas, who was a human. When he was alive we lived in Pennsylvania."

I chewed on my right thumb. I do have a lot of cousins in Pennsylvania.

"I would get to go to the North Pole?"

"Yes. We want you to interview all of Santa's reindeer because they want to set the record straight on a few things."

"Like what?"

"Like all the reindeer on Santa's team are girls," Grandma Hazel said. "It's girl power that makes Santa's sleigh fly. That and magic lichen."

"Wow! That's cool," I said. "I always thought they were boy reindeer. And what is lichen?"

"We knew you'd have a lot of questions," Grandma Hazel said. She seemed pleased. "You have the mind of a reporter. So, will you do it?"

"I have to ask my mom," I said.

"Normally that is true, but the fewer people who know about this at first, the better," Grandma Hazel said. "I can make time stand still, so when we return it will still be 7:57 p.m. on March 8. Your life will go on just as if we had never met. I will get you back safe and sound, like you never left your bedroom."

She brushed some imaginary crumbs from her skirt. "Will you do it?"

"Can I get back to you in a day or two?"

"Unfortunately, no; Santa insists that I return this evening, with or without you. It's too dangerous for me to be down here with humans."

Our golden retriever, Sir Charles, must have heard us talking because he was whining on the other side of my bedroom door.

"Is that a dog?" Grandma Hazel asked, concerned.

"Yeah. He wants in," I said.

"I like cats, but sometimes dogs can be too rough with elves," she said, and then nodded abruptly. "So, do you trust me? Will you come with me, interview the reindeer, and write the book?"

Sir Charles burst into the room. He instantly spotted Grandma Hazel, picked her up in his mouth by grabbing the back of her vest, and sped around the room.

"Sir Charles!" I yelled. "Put her down!" But he ignored me.

A Matter of Trust

Sir Charles, convinced that Grandma Hazel was some new dog toy, sped around the bedroom in circles.

"Stop!" I yelled, but it was to no avail. I thrust my arms out to block him and lunged for his collar, but he was too fast.

Finally he stopped on his own, carefully put Grandma Hazel down, sat on his haunches, and licked her face with the enthusiasm of a toddler eating his first ice cream cone.

"Oh my!" Grandma Hazel gasped.

"Are you OK? I'm sorry!" I said as I rushed to her side.

Grandma Hazel grinned. "That was quite the ride!" she said, reaching up to pat Sir Charles. "He didn't hurt me."

"That's good!" I looked at Sir Charles and pointed to the door. "Out!" I commanded. He stood up, gave me a look that said I was no fun, and slunk out the door.

Pansy had dived under the bed as soon as she saw Sir Charles, but now that he was gone she reappeared beside Grandma Hazel. Grandma Hazel petted her, assured us that she was fine, and straightened her clothes. The only evidence of the incident was slobber marks on the back of her vest.

"Now then, where were we?" she asked me. "Oh yes. Will you come and write the book?"

"I don't know," I said. "Can I think about it?"

"Unfortunately I don't have any time," Grandma Hazel said. "As you can see from the incident with Sir Charles, the human world is dangerous for me. I must return tonight. But I'd really like you to come. What is the main reason holding you back?"

I looked down at the floor. "Well, you know, 'Stranger-Danger' and 'Clever Never Goes,'" I mumbled.

"Very valid points," Grandma Hazel agreed. "It's a lot to spring on you at once. But I assure you we're related, and I am who I say I am. You're going to have to trust your instincts though."

The fact that she saw my point was reassuring, but I still wasn't convinced this was a good idea. "I don't think I can write a book," I admitted. "Sometimes I have trouble finishing things."

"It will be a challenge, but the Gallagher women have always risen to the occasion," she answered. "We don't stop trying just because something is hard."

I plopped down on the chair at my desk, and Grandma Hazel attempted to sit in my beanbag chair. She was very tiny and surrounded by moving, puffy pink vinyl. A smile escaped me as she unsuccessfully struggled to get comfortable.

I picked up a pen on my desk and drew a circle on a piece of notebook paper while considering her invitation.

"Do you remember the place in your manuscript when you wrote that the environmental crisis must be met head-on by everyone on the planet?" she asked.

I nodded.

"Emma, this is your opportunity to help in a big way," she said. "I believe a book can convince children worldwide to work together to change their habits and make environmentalism a priority in order to save Christmas and the Earth. And I believe you're the best young person for the job. As you said in your manuscript, we must all rise to the challenge."

Those very words were in my manuscript in the brown box under my bed. I picked climate change as the subject of my book because it is such a serious problem. Is destiny calling me to help solve a problem that jeopardizes the whole world?

Grandma Hazel, if that's who she really is, seems trustful. Pansy and Sir Charles like her, and Pansy is usually afraid of everything. And if

Grandma Hazel isn't who she says she is, how does she know what is in my book, and how did she get into my bedroom?

I looked across the room at my alarm clock. It still said 7:57 p.m.

I looked down at the saying on the cover of my new notebook: "When opportunity knocks, answer!"

"I'll do it," I said.

13

Beaming Up

"I guess I better go pack," I said, wondering where I had put my pink duffle bag after my last overnighter at my friend Sophia Emerson's house.

"No need," Grandma Hazel said. "I'll take care of everything. All you have to do is stand still so the beaming up goes well."

"The beaming up?"

"Yes. I just have to spread my arms a certain way, say the magic words, and you and I will be transported to Santa's Kingdom."

Grandma Hazel stood beside me. She had a beautiful, carved wooden cane in her hand that I hadn't noticed before. The carvings were of traditional Christmas things, like candles, wreaths, candy canes, snowmen, angels, and the like.

"Ready?" she asked.

I kissed the top of Pansy's head to say goodbye. "I guess." I had a feeling I wouldn't know if I was ready or not before it was too late.

She mumbled some words that were far too low for me to hear.

Suddenly I felt myself getting lighter and lighter and lighter! I looked down at my body, and it was disappearing! There was a big swoosh that was gentle but fast, like riding a Ferris wheel at top speed. Then there was nothing left but two moonbeams where Grandma Hazel and I had stood.

The next couple of minutes were a blur. It was dark, but I could see lots of stars as we flew by. Soon beautiful colors shimmered all around us. They were primarily emerald green, pink, royal blue, and purple.

Suddenly we were standing in a field of snow. The air was colder than a cherry ice pop right out of the freezer. I was wearing warm clothes, a pink ski jacket with fake fur around the hood, and a purple scarf with matching mittens. Black snow boots encased my feet. My eyelashes caught big, wet snowflakes.

"Come," Grandma Hazel said. "The kingdom was moving a bit when we transported, and instead of being inside the room I prepared for you, we'll have to walk a bit to get inside the gates."

"Why is the sky green?" I asked. I'd never seen anything like it.

"We're beyond the Northern Lights. Judging from the sky, I'd say we're about 100 miles above the Earth tonight."

It was a lot to take in. Grandma Hazel was so fast she was almost power walking, and I didn't have a chance to ask her more as I concentrated on keeping up despite all my layers of clothes. Even though it was nighttime at home, it was still twilight here.

Two male elves flanked big iron gates marking the entry to the kingdom.

"Good evening, Hazel," one of them said.

"Hello, Ronnie," Grandma Hazel replied. "We're just retiring for the evening."

"Certainly," Ronnie responded. He was a little taller than Grandma Hazel and had the same kind of pointy ears. He and his co-worker wore red hooded snowsuits with the word "Security" in big green letters across their backs.

Ronnie opened the latch with a wooden pole shaped and colored like a candy cane, and held the gate open for Grandma Hazel and me to pass. "Who is your young friend?" he asked.

"This is my granddaughter, Emma Gallagher," Grandma Hazel answered. "She is here to write a book about Santa's reindeer and the environment."

"Excellent, ma'am," Ronnie said.

Inside the gates stood houses of every color imaginable. They had lots of gables and arches, and heavy wood beams on angles nestled in their stucco walls. Their thick wooden front doors had rounded tops and big iron hinges. Most of the window panes were made of stained or etched glass.

I tried to take it all in and remember everything, because it was better than Disney World! Twinkling Christmas lights, wreaths, garlands, stars, bulbs, and bells were everywhere. The streets were deserted, but miniature snowmobiles were parked in driveways and the warm glow of lights shone in the windows. Skis, snowshoes, toboggans, and sleds leaned against some of the walls near the front doors. Snowmen and even some ice sculptures decorated some of the front lawns. There were two tiny snow angels, probably made by elf children, in front of one house. The street lights were shaped like candy canes. The Northern Lights danced high in the sky, adding another dimension to the wonderland in front of us.

Grandma Hazel led me to a pink house that looked as if it was made of candy. It was pink cotton candy-colored with white icing for its roof. A bubblegum-pink turret rose from the top floor, and the path in front was made of chocolate nonpareils candy. We entered through a front door made of candy bars with graham cracker trim. Standing in the front hallway, I could smell cinnamon and chocolate.

"It's good to be back in Santa's Kingdom," Grandma Hazel said as she pointed to a wooden peg in the hallway where I could hang up my coat.

I was too excited to be sleepy. I had never been to another country before, let alone another continent. Being on land that could float above the surface of the Earth was a new experience too.

We climbed a winding staircase. Grandma Hazel showed me to my room, which turned out to be a circular room inside the turret. It was nicer than my room at home and much tidier. There was a window seat under the window in the turret that looked like the perfect place to sit and dream. I wasn't sure where it was coming from, but I could smell vanilla.

The bedroom had a wooden, queen-size canopy bed with a white crocheted top. A blue upholstered bench sat at the foot of the bed, and two bureaus with hand-painted winter forest scenes stood along the circular walls. A large oak desk with lots of cubbyholes and an oak chair on wheels filled out the furnishings. Someone had stacked colorful notebooks and some equally colorful pens on the desk.

Grandma Hazel left me for a minute and returned with a bedtime snack of hot chocolate and Christmas sugar cookies. As I sipped the hot chocolate, she wished me "Good night and sweet dreams" and promised to see me again first thing in the morning.

The bed covers were cream-colored, down-filled, and as warm as Pansy curled up on her carpeted cat tree in the afternoon sun.

A thick, heavy white comforter lay under the bedspread. I'd never seen anything like it. Should I sleep on top of it or under it? I tried both ways and settled on it going under me.

It was like being on a puffy white cloud. Almost as soon as I closed my eyes, I was out like a shooting star.

* * * *

In the morning I discovered clothes just my size filled the bureau drawers and closet. After showering and getting dressed, I went downstairs to the kitchen and learned Grandma Hazel makes the best French toast ever.

She had cut the pieces into perfect triangles. She'd even dusted them with powdered sugar, which looked like snow on a winter prairie. The bread was thick, but the sides opposite the crust dipped down towards my plate where her knife had cut through it.

The griddle had given the bread dark brown spots like a giraffe's skin. There were smaller brown veins like frost on a windowpane near the edges. It wasn't cold though; just the opposite. It was warm, and a big glob of butter shaped like a perfect mini scoop of ice cream melted on the top.

A small pitcher of warm maple syrup sat on a white paper doily on top of a saucer. I poured some of the brown gooeyness onto the French toast, inhaled the sweet smell, and then marveled at the taste of deliciousness as the first bite slid into my mouth.

A tall glass of orange juice was next to my plate too. It had no pulp, just like I like it. I took a long drink of citrus sunshine and smacked my lips. After a breakfast like this, I was up for anything. And now I was going to get to meet Santa's reindeer!

I noticed Grandma Hazel struggling to put a dish towel on a towel bar, so I hopped up to help her. Her house was the size of a regular house and its furnishings were regular size too, which made some things hard for her to reach.

"Why is your house so big when you're so small?" I asked.

"This isn't my house, child," Grandma Hazel said. "My house is closer to the castle, on Gumdrop Avenue. This is a guest house for our human visitors."

"Do you get many human visitors?"

"I can't remember one in at least two centuries," she said. "But Santa likes to be prepared.

"My house was one of the first houses in the kingdom to use cotton candy as insulation," she added, her chin held high. "Its roof has solar panels of black licorice. Did you know solar power is now the cheapest electricity in history?

"And my house is accessible and visitable for little people or those who have trouble with steps or use wheelchairs or walkers," she added. "It helps me be independent. It has all zero-step entrances, wide doors with clear passage space, and a bathroom on the main floor that someone in a wheelchair can use. I can use all the furniture and reach all the appliances."

I poured more syrup on my French toast as Grandma Hazel got down to business.

"Now, about the environment," she said. "I've been telling Santa we were headed for a big problem with the environment since about 1850. I knew there would be trouble when the Industrial Revolution began. Santa thought things would work out fine, but they didn't.

"Now everything is messed up," she continued. "The Earth is having more heat waves, droughts, crop failures, floods, wildfires, hurricanes, and cyclones. It took me a while to convince Santa to let me reach out to you, but he eventually relented and said yes."

I cut a triangle of French toast into smaller triangles.

"The secret nature of our kingdom is crucial to preserving Christmas, so you must agree to keep our secret and not let anyone know you've visited and what you've seen here, except for the material you'll need for your book," Grandma Hazel continued. "Just tell people it was all a dream. I must take you home immediately if you can't promise to do this."

"I promise," I said. I made a big X on my chest with my right index finger to let her know I was serious, and added, "or hope to die."

"Very good," Grandma Hazel said. "We'll begin as soon as you're ready. Dasher is waiting for us in a field near the reindeer stables. You'll find her full of information and opinions. She and Dancer are the front pair on the team, and Dasher is especially organized and precise. There are some notebooks and pens on the desk in your bedroom."

I could hardly wait to meet her and get started!

Dasher

Even though it was morning, the sky still looked like twilight.

Grandma Hazel said Dasher would meet us in a field outside the reindeer barn. As we walked towards it, I could see more things in Santa's Kingdom.

The castle was spectacular. It stood in the middle of the city. The exterior was red and green, and Christmas and candy were its primary architectural styles. It had upside-down ice cream cones for turrets. There were lots of what they call "gingerbread" on Victorian homes — fancy scrolled brackets, arches, and other decorations — on all its eaves, overhangs, and crannies. In Victorian houses these things are usually made of wood, but on the castle they all seemed to be made of icing, cookies, and candy.

The wall around the castle seemed to be actual gingerbread, and white icing framed all the windows and doors. All the wooden doors were in Tudor style, with arches at the top and many big black hinges.

As we walked, we passed a sign with colorful arrows pointing in different directions. One read "Ski Resort," and I could see mountains in the distance and even a ski lift. Other signs pointed to the toy factory and the cathedral. Santa, after all, is a saint. That's why they call him Saint Nicholas.

Another sign read "Christkindlmarkt," which I think is a shopping center for Christmas ornaments, decorations, gifts, and good food. An arrow pointed to the post office, which was huge since it has to handle all those letters to Santa. There were other arrows for "The North Pole Times" and an ice skating center. I could see a lot of shops down the street from the sign that pointed to "Business District."

It would have been nice to have taken a tour of it all, but Dasher was waiting for me.

I had never seen a real reindeer before I met Dasher. I was surprised that she was smaller than I thought she'd be, as her back was only about 28 inches high. Huge antlers towered over her head though, which almost doubled her total height. They had lots of twists and turns. I wondered if she got headaches carrying all those antlers around.

"Good morning, Emma," Dasher said in a no-nonsense way. "We're glad you're here to set the record straight."

"The record?" I asked.

"Yes. Humans have a lot of misconceptions about Santa's reindeer."

"Like the fact all of the reindeer that pull Santa's sleigh are females?" I asked. "Grandma Hazel told me that last night."

"Yes. That is a key point," Dasher said. "Children are always calling us on the team 'he' when we're really all 'she.' Reindeer are the only species of deer in which the females have antlers. Female reindeer still have their antlers at Christmas, but males shed theirs as early as November, and definitely by mid-December. Females keep theirs through the winter until calving season in May. All of the paintings done of Santa's sleigh in December correctly show the reindeer have antlers, so people should know all the reindeer on Santa's team are females. Both males and females shed their antlers and grow them back each year, but at different times."

"Oh," I said, scribbling in my notebook.

"Another important point is we're closer to caribou than we are to white-tailed deer," Dasher continued, pointing to her chest with her antlers. "Do you see this ruff I have on my chest? White-tailed deer do not have big, beautiful ruffs like this. But I always see artwork where Santa's reindeer look more like white-tailed deer than real reindeer, and it's quite annoying. I think that started with how they portrayed Rudolph, but we'll talk about that later."

"I see," I said, writing as fast as possible as I tried to keep up.

"You should also know that male reindeer lose vitality during the winter, so only female reindeer are strong and healthy enough to fly a sleigh full of toys and a 250-pound elf around the world in one night," she added.

"OK," I said. "How are you able to fly, exactly? Grandma Hazel said something about lichen."

"Yes. A long time ago Santa and the elves found a magical food that allows us to fly," Dasher explained. "It's magic lichen, and it's only found here in Santa's Kingdom.

"The kind we eat is a special type of reindeer moss, but it's not really moss. Lichen isn't a plant or an animal. It's a composite organism that is usually a combination of a fungus and an algae. Sometimes it's a fungus and a cyanobacteria together. Come here; I'll show you some. We have to dig through the snow to find it. It's very high in carbohydrates."

Dasher kicked at the ground with her hooves to create a kind of crater, and uncovered a patch of a crusty, gray mass that looked a little like moss and a little like algae.

"There are a few poisonous varieties, but this is lichen that reindeer can eat," she said. "Lichen is wonderful; it can generate its own oxygen and survive out here in the cold. We must eat a lot of it to be strong enough to fly. But with climate change, there isn't enough of it. Climate change is dangerous to us reindeer, so if you can get young people interested in stopping it, it will save lives."

"That's what Grandma Hazel said I'm supposed to try to do with my book," I said.

"With global warming, ice melts into water," Dasher explained. "The water evaporates, and since the Earth is now so warm, it causes rain instead of snow. Up here, the rain freezes and we can't break through it to find the lichen to eat. More than 20,000 reindeer starved to death one year in Siberia when they couldn't break through the ice to find food. A few years later it was even worse; we lost 60,000 reindeer in a similar situation. Climate change is literally killing us up here. And it's bad for the whole planet, since everything is related."

"I'm very sorry," was all I could think of to say. It was all so tragic, and all so needless. Why didn't anyone do anything to help them before it was too late?

"We used to migrate much farther south, but our habitat has shrunk drastically since the Earth has gotten warmer. Plants and animals can't always adapt to new conditions. More than 700 mammals and birds that were on the verge of extinction in the first place are struggling the most."

I thought about that for a while. It was all so sad.

"What other things should children know about reindeer?" I asked.

"Well, if you could get them to stop putting out carrots for us on Christmas Eve, it would save us a lot of work," Dasher said. "We can't eat carrots. A piece of soft bread or grass if you have it would be much better."

"You can't eat carrots?" I asked, my eyebrows arching upwards. I had left cookies for Santa and carrots for his reindeer on a plate in our living room each Christmas Eve when I was little, when I still believed. Being a non-believer didn't seem like such a good idea now though.

"No," she said, bringing me back to the subject at hand. "We only have a bottom row of teeth; we don't have any incisor teeth that can break anything that crunchy."

"What happens to all the carrots you get then?"

"We cram them into empty toy sacks, bring them home, and give them to the Easter Bunny after Christmas," Dasher said.

"Oh," I repeated. It seemed I was saying "oh" a lot.

A minute or so passed as I went over my notes.

"What were you going to tell me about Rudolph?" I asked. "By the tone of your voice it sounded as if you might not like him much."

"He's OK," Dasher said. "I saw him and Clarice in the herd just last week. And he did save Christmas one year."

She took a moment to ponder her answer.

"I get annoyed by all the Christmas decorations I see showing the team as white-tailed deer instead of reindeer, and that's all because of how they drew Rudolph in that TV special and books," she confided in a very measured voice. "And he only led the team one night. I've been leading the team for centuries, but there's no song or TV special about me. But Rudolph went down in history!"

"You're a little jealous then, maybe?"

"Maybe a little," Dasher said. "The story of Rudolph is important because it made people more tolerant of misfits, just like I hope your book will make people want to work harder for the environment, so both the Earth and Christmas are saved."

She took a breath and continued. "The man who wrote "Rudolph" was a good guy who was just trying to help his daughter feel better. But then his story was used as a marketing ploy to get parents to buy Christmas presents at the old Montgomery Ward department stores."

"I didn't know that," I said. "I've never even heard of that store."

Dasher nodded and shook her antlers lightly. "Gone, like so many plants and animals will be if global warming continues.

"They had very good toasters," she added. I was confused until I realized she was talking about that old store.

"And speaking of toasters, Santa said everyone on the team should pick a tip to give you for the book that will help kids know how they can help," she continued. "So here is mine: turn off all electronic devices when you're not using them. By turning off your TV, DVD player, stereo, and computer when you're not using them, you'll save thousands of pounds of carbon dioxide a year.

"That's important, because carbon dioxide absorbs heat, keeping it from going into space. For the Earth's temperature to remain constant, the heat it gets from the sun must be balanced by the heat it gives off, and that's not happening these days. The hotter the Earth gets the more it destroys our food, leading to many plants and animals going extinct. There's a lot more to it, but that's how I explain it."

"You know a lot more than I do," I admitted.

"Well, I love all the STEM subjects; you know, science, technology, engineering, and math," Dasher said.

"I think science is the answer to many of our pollution problems," she continued. "Do you know that right now, some scientists are developing a new plastic that will decompose in sunlight? Promising work is being done!"

There is a lot more to Dasher than one would think. And I might not be able to get all this down in a book.

Dasher looked at me intently. "Santa said humans have trouble believing things they don't understand," she said. "He said I should give you a ride to prove that his reindeer can fly. I have his permission to use some lichen for a short flight. Would you like that?"

I could feel my eyes getting wide. "Yes!" I nodded, clapping my hands in anticipation.

The Ride

"OK," Dasher said. "Stay here, and I'll be back in a couple of minutes."

When she returned she was wearing a red saddle. It had a triangular front that was higher than the rest of it. Two spaces were cut out of the front to provide places to hold. Stirrups dangled on both sides of her back.

"Do you see that fence?" Dasher asked, pointing with her antlers. "Can you climb onto the second rail, and then slide onto the saddle? You'll be sitting more on my shoulders than my back. I'll move as close as I can to the fence for you."

I did as she directed, skipped over to the fence, climbed onto it, and slid my right leg over her back. My weight didn't faze her.

Once I was aboard, with my feet in the stirrups and my hands holding onto the front of the saddle, Dasher said to reach along the sides of the saddle and find a seat belt. "Buckle it around your waist, and then hold onto the front of the saddle with your hands," she instructed. "There are goggles on a cord attached to the saddle; take them off the cord and put them on too. Try not to move too much; just relax and sway as I sway."

I tried to do as I was told. I could feel my heart beating quicker and quicker, and I couldn't stop smiling.

There wasn't much time to think, but I did wonder if she would run down the field faster and faster and then take off like an airplane. I quickly learned that's not how reindeer take flight.

Instead, Dasher started to hop around quickly.

"Hold on tight!" she instructed.

My neck snapped back and forth with each hop like I was on a bucking bronco. My stomach hopped too, a couple of seconds behind my neck.

Dasher's hops became leaps, and the leaps got bigger and bigger. I was about to yell to her that we could skip the ride when suddenly we were airborne. We rose higher and higher within seconds.

It was simultaneously exhilarating and terrifying.

"Wow! I'm flying!" I shouted. "Whee!"

The reindeer barn got smaller as Dasher and I circled the field above it. I sat as still as possible and bent a little at the waist. I gripped the front of the saddle tightly. The icy wind whipped us both.

"How are you doing?" Dasher yelled.

"I'm fine, I think!" I couldn't believe I was flying, let alone flying on one of Santa's reindeer over the top of the world.

I shivered and my teeth chattered. I was glad for the goggles and my waterproof coat and pants when little pieces of ice bounced off us. They stung when they hit the parts of my face that the goggles, hat and scarf didn't cover.

Dasher gained even more altitude, and my stomach churned as the snowy landscape got even smaller. I could hear Dasher pant a little from the exertion, and our breath made vapor clouds in the cold air.

We flew in a large circle. I could see the colorful spires and turrets of Santa's Kingdom below us. Beyond the kingdom were only glaciers and the sea.

"We'll head back down now; continue to hold on tight!" Dasher said, and we started to descend.

Although the take-off had been bumpy, the landing was very smooth. Once she was back on Earth, Dasher ran along the ground for a bit before she stopped right back at the fence. I didn't need it to dismount though, because once she stopped and I unbuckled, I slid off.

"That was wonderful! Thank you!"

Dasher nodded and pointed her antlers towards the reindeer barn, where Grandma Hazel was waiting for me.

"How did you like your ride, dear?" she asked.

"It was wonderful!" I repeated, exhilarated. "I can't believe I rode a flying reindeer!"

"It was very nice of Dasher to give you a ride," Grandma Hazel said. "I hope you thanked her."

"Oh, yes! She was very nice, and she knows a lot about science!"

"Did you learn some things about sustainability?"

My eyes lowered as my exhilaration plummeted into worry.

"I didn't get all the stuff she told me about carbon dioxide down," I admitted. "It's kind of complicated."

"It's a complicated problem, with no easy answers," Grandma Hazel agreed. "That's partly why people avoid addressing it, but if they realized how serious it is and that there are small steps they can make in their everyday lives to help solve it, we'd be able to make a big difference."

"And that's where I come in?" I asked, looking doubtful.

"Dasher is serious and businesslike; I think you'll find Dancer more fun."

Dancer

I was to meet Dancer inside the reindeer barn. Like the other buildings in Santa's Kingdom, it was in Tudor style. It had dark brown wood for accents over cream stucco. I later found out that what I thought was wood was straight pretzel sticks dipped in chocolate, and the stucco was hardened meringue frosting.

I slid one side of the large front doors open and Grandma Hazel and I walked inside. It was bright, cheerful, and warm. I was glad the barn was heated, because my flight had been so cold.

There were roomy stalls on both sides of a long concrete aisle. The stalls were full of cedar shavings, which made the whole building smell spicy. There were Christmas wreaths with red ribbons and white balls on each sliding stall door, and all the doors were open. In addition to the cedar, I could smell something like cloves and ginger. The scents intermingled like some sort of heavenly bakery.

Suddenly, however, loud Brazilian music came pouring out of loudspeakers somewhere overhead, and Dancer came dancing down the aisle doing the samba.

A purple scarf was wrapped around her forehead, just below where her antlers began. It covered her ears and looked like a turban. About 100 big, gold, hoop earrings dangled from the tines of her antlers. A magenta skirt with lots of white flounces was belted around her middle from her belly to her spine. She also wore about 50 purple, green, and gold Mardi Gras beads as necklaces.

I tried not to laugh, but a giggle escaped.

"Hello, Emma! I'm Dancer, and I love to dance!" she sang as she approached me. "Do you know how to samba? I can teach you!"

"That's OK," I said quickly.

"There are three steps to two beats," she said as if she hadn't heard me. "It's one uh two, three uh four, five uh six, seven uh eight. You have to bend and straighten your knees and then you bounce," she proclaimed, again letting the word "bounce" flow out as if it were bigger than any other word in the sentence. "Let's see you move! Swing your hips! Twist and tap!"

"That's OK," I repeated, but I gave it a try.

My lack of talent didn't slow Dancer down. She danced up and down the aisle while the song played on the loudspeakers and I tried to keep up. As she danced I noticed a clicking sound, like she might be following the beat of the music by playing castanets.

"OK, Benny; I guess that's it for a while," she called to someone named Benny, and the music stopped.

She trotted over to me, and I realized Grandma Hazel had disappeared. But the clicking continued, so I asked Dancer about it.

"Ah! It's not castanets; it's because we reindeer make a clicking noise when we walk," she explained. "We have tendons that snap over certain bones in our feet, which makes the clicking noise. Listening for the clicks helps us stay together in a herd, especially in snowstorms or when it's foggy."

"That's amazing," I said.

"Yes!" she said. "It's even in a song; you know, click, click, click!"

I didn't know what she meant. Then a lightbulb went off in my head.

"Oh! Up on the housetop! Click, click, click! Down through the chimney with old Saint Nick!" I sang.

"That's right!" she said, pleased.

A few beats passed, and she changed the subject.

"I understand you talked to Dasher," Dancer said. "She said she told you many things about reindeer and climate change."

"Yes."

"Dasher and I are feminists," she announced. "We think girls don't get enough credit for all the wonderful things we can do. She and I both love the STEM subjects.'

"She did mention that," I said.

"Did she tell you about our wonderful eyes?" Dancer asked, making hers big and rolling them around on her face. "We can see ultraviolet light better than other animals. That helps us see even white things like polar bears in the snow."

"I didn't know that," I said, making another note in my notebook. "I'm learning a lot."

"That's wonderful!" Dancer said. "Santa said we're supposed to give you our favorite conservation tip. I had to think about that for a long time because there are so many!"

"What did you come up with?"

"Well, I have a lot of lightbulbs around my dressing table, so my tip will be about lightbulbs," she said. "Many people have already replaced their regular lightbulbs with LED lightbulbs, but some remain. Please tell the children that if they can get their parents to use only LED lightbulbs, it will save lots of carbon dioxide and help the environment!

"Plus, it will save money. And when we save money on utilities, we have more money to spend on dancing lessons, music, and jewelry!" She shook her antlers, making her gold earrings clink.

"Well, OK then," I said, nodding.

"In general, new products save more energy than old products do, so it's usually better to buy a new product than to fix an old product in the long run," she added. "You have to consider the energy savings in addition to the basic cost of the item when you're deciding what product to buy."

Dancer batted her eyes at me. "Can I add one more thing?"

I nodded.

"Tell the kids to learn as much as possible about wind power and windmills!" she said. "Wind power is one of the fastest-growing renewable energy technologies!

"It was so nice talking to you!" Dancer did the samba as she danced away from me. "I have to go work on my choreography now!"

Prancer

As Dancer sambaed her way around a corner and out of view, the music coming from the loudspeakers stopped, and the barn fell silent. I went into one of the empty stalls and sat down on two bags of cedar shavings. Even through the brown paper bags the shavings smelled heavy and rich, like Mom's cedar chest where she keeps blankets and quilts.

It was quiet until I heard something rustling overhead. Soon the rustling stopped, and a tiny body climbed down a ladder from the loft overhead into the stall where I sat.

"Hi, Emma!" an elf said. "My name is Benny. I'm one of the elves who work with the reindeer to ensure they're happy and healthy."

Benny was about the same size as Grandma Hazel and had ears like hers. He wore a green tunic, green-and-white striped leggings, a green-and-white stocking cap with a white puff at the end of it, and shiny black boots. I noticed a tiny checkered flag pin on the lower edge of his cap.

"Hi, Benny," I said. "It's very nice to meet you."

"Likewise, I'm sure," Benny replied. "I guess Prancer is your next interview. You have some time because she's always late."

"Why is that?"

"I think she feels entitled, after the big blow-out of 1927. But you don't know anything about that, do you?"

"No," I admitted. "What happened?"

Benny sat down on a bag of shavings next to me and talked in a hushed voice.

"Well, Prancer and Vixen are paired on the team, so they must work well together," he said. "Prancer was responsible for collecting money for our Christmas cookie drive that year. Somehow more than $500 went missing! Prancer said she gave it to Vixen, but Vixen said she never got it. She said Prancer was framing her, and that Prancer had to have stolen the money. Bad words were said between them, and they had been best friends!" Benny shook his head and looked down at the floor.

"Oh my!" I said, opening my notebook.

"Yes," Benny went on. "It was like a soap opera. At first they yelled at each other, and then they wouldn't speak to each other, and then they got to yelling again. It caused a lot of problems for the team. One day it got so bad they had a physical fight, and Vixen knocked off Prancer's right antler!"

"She didn't?" I said, shocked.

Benny nodded. "So not only was Prancer still upset, but she had a headache for months since she had to walk around lopsided all the time. As you may know, compared to their body size, reindeer have the largest and heaviest antlers of all species of deer."

"That must have hurt when it got knocked off too," I said.

"Having an antler only on one side didn't help her attitude. They eventually grew back fine, but it was awful for a while."

"Was the money ever found?"

"Yes; it turned up in a pocketbook that Vixen had been using but then put away in her closet. Vixen did say she was sorry, but Prancer wouldn't accept her apology. Santa spoke to them both, but it didn't help. He was almost ready to replace them, but finally Cupid convinced Prancer to forgive Vixen so they could continue to work together. They are at least cordial to each other now."

"That's quite a story," I said, writing it down.

"Here Prancer comes; I hear her prancing towards us. Later!" Benny disappeared.

Prancer came clicking down the aisle and gracefully sat down.

She had perfect posture. A red and green Hermès scarf circled her neck. Oversized, black plastic sunglasses were clipped onto the scarf with one of their earpieces.

"How do you do, Emma?" she said. "May I introduce myself? My name is Prancer."

"I'm very pleased to meet you," I said. "I understand you prance a lot, but how did you get your name?"

She paused and then quietly said, "It was given to me by my parents at birth. But I don't just prance; I do dressage."

"Dressage?"

"Yes; it's a type of horse-riding competition, but reindeer can do it too if they're so inclined to learn," Prancer said. "It's a French word, and it means 'training.' It's a form of art."

"Like drawing?" I said, confused.

"No, like ballet," Prancer explained in a very measured and calm way. "It's a complex program of specialized movements, sometimes done to music. I began to study it after a personal problem, and I've been told my extended trot is quite beautiful," she said matter-of-factly.

"Was the personal problem the fact that money went missing from the Christmas cookie drive, and there was a big fight that caused you to lose half of your antlers?"

Prancer closed her eyes, took a deep breath, and opened her eyes. A heater somewhere switched on, blowing warm air. She wet her lips and then lifted her head a few inches.

"Yes, but I had to move on and forgive Vixen because Santa can't do without me on the team," she said with quiet dignity.

"That must have been hard," I said.

"Yes. Vixen was in hot water for a long time, but I had to learn to forgive her and move on so I could resume enjoying my own life," Prancer said.

"I'm so glad you were able to," I answered.

"Yes. I had to find a way to prance on," Prancer said. "Cupid taught me that important lesson."

She smiled at me.

"Now, speaking of hot water, Santa said we are to give you tips to pass on to the children about conservation, so we can continue to find enough magic lichen to eat so we can fly," she said. "My tip has to do with hot water."

"That's funny, considering," I said.

Prancer didn't smile. "My tip is to use less of it," she said. "The average person uses 100 gallons of water daily, which could easily be reduced.

"Don't let the water run while you're brushing your teeth," she suggested. "If you have one, use a dishwasher instead of hand-washing dishes. Let your dishes air dry when the cycle completes, too.

"Also, it takes a lot of energy to heat water, so if you can think of ways to not heat so much of it, it will help.

"For example, you can use less hot water by taking shorter and cooler showers," she said.

"Your family can also wash clothes in cold or warm water instead of hot water," she added. "If everyone would do it, it would save a great deal of energy."

I'm glad Prancer and Vixen were able to patch things up. Her story made me curious about Vixen.

Vixen

I didn't have to wonder what Vixen was like for long.

"She's having a pedicure; you can find her in the reindeer spa at the other end of the barn," Benny told me, and gave me directions.

As I walked, I came across big doors leading to another area. Hoping to find Santa's sleigh inside, I pushed the doors open, but it was just a feed room filled with bags of grain and bales of hay. I would really like to see that sleigh. After all, how could it possibly hold toys for all the children in the world?

I continued to walk and soon discovered Vixen standing in the center of a white-tiled room with each of her feet planted in a footbath powered by solar panels. Wispy steam from the four footbaths enveloped her, and six elves surrounded her. Two white ladders which they must have used to climb onto her leaned on either side of her body.

One elf trimmed the hair around her ears. One applied conditioner to her ruff while another brushed it with a pink brush that said "Cutie Pie" in script lettering done in rhinestones. One had his hands in one of the footbaths and seemed to be adjusting the water temperature amidst the bubbles. Two others were massaging her back.

Slow, relaxing music drifted in from somewhere, and the scent of strong incense hung in the air. I think it was patchouli.

A tiny, tan Pekingese dog slept soundly in a pastel pink dog bed in the corner of the room. Vixen sighed and smiled when she noticed me.

"You must be Emma," she cooed. "They told me you were coming. Welcome, child."

"Thank you." I took my notebook out of my pocket and wondered what to ask her first.

"Thank you, Maurice; that temperature is splendid," she told an elf who had his hands in one of the footbaths. He nodded and dumped more of what looked like Epsom salts into the water.

"It's important to take care of your feet," Vixen told me. "Do you know we reindeer have special hooves?"

"I did not know that," I said.

"Yes, in the summer, when the ground is wet, our foot pads are soft so we have extra grip. In the winter they tighten up, and the rim of our hooves are exposed. That gives us extra traction in the snow and ice."

"I did not know that," I repeated.

"Stick with me, dear, and I'll show you the ropes," Vixen said, batting her long, fake eyelashes. "It's important to take care of your legs; some of us reindeer migrate up to 3,000 miles a year."

"I did not know that," I said a third time.

"Baby oil; that's one of my tricks," Vixen confided. "It helps keep my legs smooth and silky. I think my legs are one of my best features."

I didn't know what to say to that, so I took a different approach.

"So, Vixen, what do you do for fun?" I asked, hoping to get to know her better before she shared her environmental tips with me.

"Well, I love to migrate and see new places," she said. "When the weather is bad I enjoy board games, especially strategy games like Cuboro Tricky Ways and mahjong. When the weather permits, I enjoy going to new restaurants and shopping. I also enjoy the jazz clubs."

"I didn't realize you had so many options up here at the North Pole," I said.

"Oh yes; we're quite worldly," Vixen replied. "I get all the fashion magazines, and try to stay on top of things.

"Plus, I like to think I'm sort of a gourmet," she added. "We reindeer have four stomachs, you know. I like to keep up on which restaurants offer the best beet pulp, and dried and fresh willow leaves."

I wondered if it was OK to mention the fight. I decided to go ahead, even though Vixen's eyes were closed as the elves continued their treatments.

"I was told you and Prancer fought over some misplaced money, which affected both of your positions on the team," I said.

A few measures of the music passed, and Vixen slowly opened her eyes.

"Ancient history," she said, dismissing the whole topic.

"Santa said we were each to give you a conservation tip for your book," Vixen said, pushing ahead. "Here is mine. Adjust your thermostat. Moving it down just 2 degrees in winter and up 2 degrees in summer is an easy, tricky way to save energy. A programmable thermostat is great for that; you can just set it once and forget it."

"I did not know that," I repeated one more time.

"I know I'm just supposed to give you one tip, but I have to mention solar energy," she added. "There's far more to it than just giving us good tans.

"Solar energy converts power from the sun into thermal or electrical energy. It's the cleanest and most abundant renewable energy source. There are programs that make the prices for solar panels for homes more affordable than they've been in the past. Kids should learn about it and talk to their parents about it. Up here, we use it as much as possible. Even my footbaths are solar-powered."

"That's interesting," I said, and suddenly Grandma Hazel appeared.

"Let's say goodbye and go back to the house," she said. "We're dining with Santa and Mrs. Claus tonight."

Dinner with Santa

Every kid has dreamed of visiting Santa Claus at the North Pole. I'm doing it! What will he be like? What will his castle be like? I hope he likes me! This is an amazing opportunity! What should I wear?

I followed Grandma Hazel's advice and chose a forest-green jumper and a white blouse with little red-and-white candy canes. I wore white tights under it, and black flats. I put my hair up in my usual ponytail, but I wrapped it with a fancy red bow I found in my top dresser drawer, like it had been put there just for me.

Grandma Hazel wore a long red-plaid dress with a white sweater. She had a poinsettia pin on, and black patent-leather shoes. She wore a red earring on the side of her head with green hair, and a green earring on the side of her head with red hair.

I think we both looked nice.

Dinner was in the private dining room of Santa's castle. It was even bigger than my school's cafeteria, and much fancier. A fire blazed in a gray stone fireplace that took up almost one end of the room. A large painting of the nativity scene hung above the fireplace. A grandfather clock with elaborate wood carvings on its face ticked away close to the fireplace.

Thanks to the blazing fire, the room smelled like bonfires and fall. A dozen lighted red candles in two silver candelabras on the heavy, dark-wood mantle made the room smell like wax and cinnamon too.

The other three walls had heavy wooden bookcases filled with examples of what was manufactured in Santa's toy factory. When

I asked Grandma Hazel about them, she said each toy represented was one of the most-requested toys in its category.

The electronics section had all the latest video games, toys, and accessories, including a set of earbuds I got last Christmas and some games that were so new I don't think they are even in stores yet. I wondered how that was even possible!

I moved closer to Grandma Hazel, because it was intimidating to be in a room that was so elegant. A huge wooden dining table surrounded by wooden chairs stood in the center of the room. The table was set with white china with circles of green garland and red-and-white candy canes along the rims of the plates and saucers. Heavy red napkins with green holly napkin rings were on the left side of each dinner plate. The silverware was heavy and had reindeer on the top of each piece. The glasses were fragile and trimmed with the same garland and candy canes used on the dinnerware.

I learned it would be a party of five: Mr. and Mrs. Claus; Grandma Hazel and me, and a tall, thin man named Robert Strauss. He was the editor of "The North Pole Times," and Grandma Hazel said he would help edit my manuscript when it was ready.

Mr. Strauss, Grandma Hazel, and I had arrived first. Mr. Strauss wore a lilac shirt that complemented his gray hair. His bluish-gray eyes twinkled under his eyeglasses.

"Hello, ladies!" he said with a big smile. "Don't you look beautiful tonight?

"And you must be Emma; I'm so glad to meet you!" he said, nodding and smiling so big I automatically smiled back. He shook my hand like I was a grown-up and then touched my arm slightly. "I understand you're a wonderful young writer who has accepted the challenge to write a book about our plight. I will help in any way I can!"

"Thank you!" I said sincerely. "I need as much help as possible."

"I have something here for you that should help," Mr. Strauss said, and he handed me a flat box wrapped in lilac paper with a big white ribbon and a big white bow.

"Thank you!" I said, and then I unwrapped the present. Under the tissue paper in the box was a beautiful new briefcase. It wasn't your typical briefcase like grown-ups have, but more like a flat folder with handles.

"Every star writer needs a good briefcase!" Mr. Strauss said.

"Thank you!" I repeated, but I didn't have time to talk anymore just then because Santa and Mrs. Claus were entering through the big wooden dining room doors! I had never met anyone as important and famous as Santa Claus. It was a lot to take in, especially since so many of my friends were convinced Santa and Mrs. Claus didn't exist, and they had convinced me too. I thought about the boys in the back of my school bus who had first told me Santa Claus was just a myth. Ha!

Santa looked just like his pictures, except he wore casual clothes and not a red fur-trimmed suit. He wore brown tweed pants, a long-sleeved tan suede shirt, and a dark brown vest that covered his big belly. He did have boots on, but they were brown ones like men wear inside a house, not black snow boots.

His blue eyes were brighter than I thought they'd be. They looked like the brightest blue you could ever see, and they twinkled when he smiled. He did have a beard as white as snow too.

Mrs. Claus wore a long green skirt with a red sweater. Her long silver hair was up in a bun. Like her husband, she wore wire-framed eyeglasses, only hers were silver and his were gold. She greeted everyone with a hug.

It was clear that both Santa and Mrs. Claus wanted everyone to be happy. And just like in that poem, "A Visit from St. Nicholas" by Clement Clarke Moore, I did laugh a little when I saw him in spite of myself. My giggles were mostly from excitement and nerves though.

Don't be star-struck! You are here to do a job!

How can we convince kids to take better care of the environment? What should I say in the book? Do you think this will even work?

Questions spun around in my head, but it wouldn't be polite to bombard Santa with them at dinner.

I will have to try to work them into the conversation naturally. But how?

"Ah, they're pulling out all the stops for you," Grandma Hazel whispered as the first course of what turned out to be a complete, traditional Christmas dinner was served. Later, when the turkey platter was passed, I noticed she didn't put any meat on her plate. "Along with being kind to animals, it's better for the environment," she said in a low voice that only I could hear.

Santa asked me if I liked the Easy-Bake oven he gave me when I was 6. Luckily I remembered it, and I thanked him for it. He said he was pleased that I had always been on his good list. He said he was glad I was a good reader, and complimented me on getting my math test scores up. The fact he knew all of this about me was a little weird, but then again, he was Santa!

He said to thank my dad for getting our chimney cleaned annually. "Regular cleanings make it safer for the entire family, and more pleasant for me," he pointed out. "It's also good for the air quality and the environment."

I desperately wanted to ask him how he visited all the children in the world on Christmas Eve, but I couldn't see any way to work that into the conversation.

He asked me how I was enjoying meeting his reindeer, and I answered truthfully. "They're incredible, and it's a once-in-a-lifetime opportunity I'll never forget," I said. "I'm learning a lot."

Things were going well, but without thinking I blurted out a question. "Can I see your sleigh?"

Santa looked surprised, and everyone stopped talking. The only sound was the ticking of the grandfather clock near the fireplace.

"Ho, ho, ho!" Santa said a few seconds later. "I think we need to keep a few things a secret," he answered. I was worried, but then I was sure he wasn't mad because he winked.

Santa looked at me intently. "You know, Emma, I hesitated to invite you here because I think writing a book is a tall order for anyone, let alone one so young," he said. "But your great-grandmother and my reindeer can be quite convincing. There are three things I'd like for you to remember to tell the other children when you're writing it."

"What are those three things, Santa?" Grandma Hazel asked for me.

"The first one is that many of the things that need to be done to clean up our environment are things that don't take a lot of effort," Santa answered. "Humans have developed bad habits in their everyday routines that they must break."

"Very true, Santa," Grandma Hazel agreed, and everyone at the table nodded.

"To break a bad habit, first you have to want to change it, and that's where I hope you can help us, Emma," he continued. "We need to show children the importance of doing things differently, and make them want to do it. We need them to have more gumption!"

I had never heard the word "gumption" before, and it made me giggle.

"I'm sorry, Santa; what is gumption?" I asked.

Santa stroked his beard as he thought. "Yes, it is a funny word, isn't it? It means spunk! It is when you are determined not to give up. You must have initiative and resourcefulness and even courage, because sometimes it takes courage to undertake difficult things."

"I think I like that word," I said.

"Well, if humans would have the gumption to change their bad habits, they would take the small steps necessary to turn a bad habit into a good one," Santa continued. "Sometimes they throw something away that they could have recycled because they just don't think about the better option. They need to think about the choices they're making. It's more about substituting a new practice for an old one. And kids can help the adults change their ways!

"Once someone makes a better choice one time, it becomes easier. And when other people join in, it becomes easier for everyone. Do you see what I mean?"

"Yes. I understand, Santa," I said.

"Another thing I want to point out is that lives depend on it," Santa said. "I don't think anyone wants Christmas to disappear, but that's what we're facing if we don't have the magic lichen to help my reindeer fly.

"But that's not all. Climate change is too hard on many animals and plants. They just can't adapt. Right now coral, polar bears, and frogs come to mind, but many animals and plants are already on the verge of extinction and they won't be around anymore if changes aren't made. In the case of polar bears, which of course are important to us here at the North Pole, global warming causes rising temperatures that melt the sea ice, so the bears have to work harder to catch food, which puts their survival at risk."

Santa took a big breath. "God made all of the plants and the animals, and they all have a role to play. Tragically, we have already lost some."

Everyone at the table looked sad.

"The third thing I want to point out is that it will take teamwork," Santa continued. "My entire kingdom is built on teamwork. The elves work together to make the toys. The elves in the mail department work together to keep the lists updated. There are elves to care for Mrs. Claus, the other elves, the reindeer, and me.

"None of us could do what we do at Christmas individually, but together we're a mighty force," he said, his voice rising on the last two words. "Just like everyone works as a team at the North Pole and just like my reindeer work together to fly me around the world to make my deliveries on Christmas Eve, it will take everyone pulling together to clean up the environment, and we must do it now before all is lost.

"Habits are much easier to form if you want to change something," he added. "If each kid does just one small thing for conservation, it will make him or her want to do another small thing. And if everyone does small things, together we'll make a difference. But making everyone want to start is vital."

I looked up at the ceiling and then down at my plate. I bit my lower lip and then smiled at him weakly.

Comet

I was halfway through meeting the reindeer team, and first thing the next morning I met Comet. I thought she might have gotten that name because she could run and fly fast, but instead it was because she loves astronomy.

She was waiting for Grandma Hazel and me outside the reindeer barn, right on time.

"Howdy! Very pleased to meet you!" she said in a Southern drawl.

"Likewise," I said. With four interviews to do today I didn't have any time to waste, but I postponed question number one on my list because I had to know something. "Why do you have a Southern accent?" I asked.

"Ah, honey, it's funny you should mention that," she said in her long, drawn-out way. "It's because my ancestors were originally from Nashville in the great state of Tennessee."

"Reindeer in Tennessee?" I asked. "Isn't it too warm there for reindeer?"

"Yes, ma'am," she said, nodding hard enough that her antlers bobbed up and down. "I'm a descendant of the caribou that ranged as far south as Tennessee during the Pleistocene Epoch."

I wondered if she was just kidding me. "When was that?"

"About 2.6 million years ago," she said without hesitation. "That's when the most recent Ice Age occurred, and glaciers were everywhere!"

"Oh," I said. "And you know that because?"

"Because I like genealogy, cosmology, paleontology, and really all the ologies," Comet replied. "Once I learned where my family came from, I did some more studying and learned about the Southern way of life. Now I talk Southern, think Southern, and cook Southern. And I love country music!"

"Oh!" I said, surprised. "Who is your favorite country singer?"

"Oh, I love all of them, darlin'!" she said. "I like Alan Jackson, Reba McEntire, Garth Brooks, Billy Dean, George Strait, Brad Paisley, Blake Shelton, Tim McGraw and Faith Hill, Martina McBride, Lady A, Kenny Chesney, Keith Urban, Luke Bryan, Dolly Parton, Hank Williams Jr., Sugarland, and Luke Combs."

"That's a lot of singers," I said.

Comet giggled.

Then she moved closer and lowered her voice. "Speaking of strange, you have an interesting family. Do you know who one of your ancestors was?"

"Well, Grandma Hazel," I said. "She's the only ancestor I've ever met." I looked around, but Grandma Hazel had disappeared.

"And what is your last name, Miss Emma?" Comet asked.

"Gallagher." Where was this going?

"Ah, a good Irish name," Comet said, nodding. "It makes perfect sense."

"What does?"

"Well, she might not have told you this, but your Grandma Hazel, and therefore you too, are related to the leprechauns from Ireland who have pots of gold at the end of rainbows!"

"Wow!"

"Yes." She nodded. "It's all very interesting, especially since there are no girl leprechauns."

"There aren't?"

"No," she said. "And leprechauns are an endangered species."

"I've been learning a lot about endangered species with this assignment I have," I said.

"I'm sure you have, sugar," Comet said. "There's even a new science for that, called conservation biology. You know all about our magic lichen, but many plants and animals are at risk. The animals up here that are in the most danger seem to be the polar bears, but there are animals all over the world that might become extinct if their native habitat is ruined by humans. I know some of them: snow leopards, giant pandas, tigers, elephants, gorillas, cheetahs, green sea turtles, and even monarch butterflies."

"That's terrible," I said. I thought about how awful it would be to lose all those animals. "It would be terrible if any of them became extinct."

"I know, darlin', and that's why we're all hoping your book will help convince kids to take conservation and the environment seriously.

"I'm very into recycling," she added. "You must have met Robert Strauss, the editor of 'The North Pole Times'? Well, I write a column about recycling for the paper every month, and I organize a big garage sale each summer.

"And that brings me to my tip," she said. "Please ask the children to recycle more. They can recycle products and lots of their household waste. They could even make crafts from some of the things they recycle!

"Kids need to help the grown-ups make better choices," she emphasized. "They can suggest their parents use dryer balls instead of dryer sheets. Anything that cuts down on waste is good. For example, hand blowers in restrooms are better than paper towels.

"I hate litter," she added. "I don't know why people throw things out of their car windows instead of putting garbage in the trash. Not only is litter terrible for the environment, it just looks ugly!

"I do like the practice of composting very much," she went on. "A compost pile doesn't take up much space in the backyard, and it helps the ground and the grass.

"Each year people produce more than 400 million tons of plastic garbage," she said. "400 million tons is a lot!

"One thing that would help would be for people to stop buying bottled water. Use reusable water bottles, filters, and tap water instead. That would save packaging and energy.

"Recycling is easy and very important, y'all!" she concluded.

"Those are all excellent tips," I said.

"I'm so glad you liked them!" Comet responded. "I have to go fry up a mess of collard greens now," she added as she trotted away. "Holler if you need me!"

And just like that, Grandma Hazel reappeared.

"Are we really related to leprechauns?" I asked her.

She smiled but didn't reply.

Cupid

I suspected Cupid would be nice since she was able to get Prancer to forgive Vixen for that misplaced money.

Suddenly she stood in front of us. She had an aura of confidence about her, and she was stunning. She wasn't an albino, but she had more white hair than tan hair, which made her stand out.

She was petite as reindeer go, but she had large antlers. Mistletoe was threaded around each point, giving her a very festive look. A silver heart locket that had "Love Bug" engraved in script letters on its side draped around her neck. A white lace hanky was tied into her ruff. She also wore pink eyeglasses with pink lenses in the shape of hearts. She smelled like expensive perfume.

"I'm so sorry; I was in our solar-powered hot tub, and time got away from me," Cupid said. "I hope you weren't waiting long?"

"Not at all," I said. "I'm Emma, and I guess you know Grandma Hazel."

"Yes, I do, and it's very nice to meet you, Emma," Cupid said politely. "Shall we go into the barn and have some tea?"

We went through the big front doors, and Grandma Hazel and I followed Cupid into her stall. All the stalls in the reindeer barn were as big as bedrooms. Hers had cedar shavings on the floor, but it also had lace curtains on the windows and a circular wooden table in the middle with two chairs. A Christmas tea set waited for us on top of a thick white tablecloth. Another matching teapot stood on a matching plate. The rest of the table held a large plate of Christmas cookies; three plates for us; shiny, heavy silverware, and luxurious white cloth napkins with silver napkin rings.

"Shall I pour?" Grandma Hazel said.

"Thank you, yes," Cupid said. "I can do it, but it's easier for someone with fingers and thumbs. We have a choice of tea or hot chocolate."

Cupid and Grandma Hazel chose the tea. I picked the hot chocolate, and Grandma Hazel poured for all of us. There were even marshmallows in a sugar bowl for my hot chocolate.

"So, you're almost 12, and you enjoy writing, I'm told?" Cupid asked me.

I nodded as I bit into a fancy green cookie that had been made with a cookie press.

"That's wonderful," Cupid answered. "Who is your teacher at school, and do you have a sweetheart?"

"Mrs. Morgan is my teacher, and no, I don't like anyone that way," I said.

"That will change," Cupid told me as she and Grandma Hazel smiled at each other. I looked down at my plate.

"What do you do for fun?" I asked.

"I love archery," Cupid said. "It's a wonderful sport. We have targets set up behind the barn. I also like to do embroidery and to read. I love poetry, especially love sonnets."

"That's nice," I said.

"Cupid has won many awards for her archery skills," Grandma Hazel told me.

"You're very kind," Cupid said. "I also love Valentine's Day," she added. "I make handmade greeting cards throughout the year, and I make sure all the elves get a Valentine card from the reindeer team each February 14th."

"That's nice too," I said.

"Yes. I supply extras and suggest certain elves send them to other certain elves on that holiday," she added.

"Cupid is the kingdom's matchmaker," Grandma Hazel told me.

"Like Christmas, Valentine's Day is a wonderful holiday," Cupid answered. "Love can conquer all, you know, and I hope the children love the Earth enough to want to save it."

"What is your tip?" I asked.

"Well, although I admit I like packaged goods like makeup, perfume, and other nice things, my tip is to avoid products with a lot of packaging," she said. "Some experts have said it can take 150 years for some of that foamy white packaging to break down in a landfill. That's a long time! It's essential to keep everything we can out of landfills in the first place, especially packaging we don't really need.

"Parents and children can write to companies to ask them to clearly label what part of their packaging can be recycled," she continued. "That would remove any doubts and remind people to recycle simultaneously. And of course we can ask companies to change to more biodegradable packaging."

"What does that mean?" I asked.

"Biodegradable? It means something that can be decomposed by bacteria or other living organisms," she explained. "Biodegradable packaging can be broken down into smaller pieces and reabsorbed into the environment, ideally without causing any pollution."

"I see," I said.

"As consumers, we can pick products with less packaging over products with a lot of it," Cupid continued. "We can bring our own reusable bags to the grocery store too. There is a lot we can do that's not hard. We just have to want to try!"

Getting kids to want to try was where my book would come in. I looked at Cupid and wondered how I would ever pull it off.

Benny

Grandma Hazel and I ran into Benny when we were approaching the barn's big front doors following Cupid's tea party.

"Hello ladies!" Benny said while he juggled a large Christmas wreath he was carrying.

I had been wanting to ask him something since I met him, and now seemed to be as good a time as any.

"Hi Benny!" I said. "Could I ask you something?"

"Sure! Just let me put this wreath down," he said. "There must be a short, because some of the bulbs aren't lighting. I'm going to see if I can repair it in our shop. What can I do for you?"

"Nothing, really. I just wanted to ask you about the checkered flag you have on your cap. I'm a big racing fan."

"You are? That's terrific!" Benny said enthusiastically. "What kind of racing do you like best?"

"My whole family loves sprint car racing," I said. "We go to as many races in the summer as we can."

"Wonderful!" Benny said. "Well, I do a little racing myself, but I race snowmobiles, not sprint cars."

"You do? Wow! How cool!"

Grandma Hazel spoke up then. "Benny is being modest," she said. "He is a multi-time snowmobile champion."

"Wow!" I repeated. "Can I see your snowmobiles and your shop?"

"Sure!" Benny said, smiling at us both. "I don't have to fix this wreath right now. I could take you for a little ride, if it's OK with your grandma."

"Wow!" I repeated one more time. "Really? I've never been on a snowmobile!"

"That would be fine," Grandma Hazel said. "I'll go back to the guest house. Just bring her back there before dark. Emma, I'll postpone your last two interviews. I'm sure that will be fine."

Benny's snowmobile shop was a quick walk from the barn, and I was amazed at how big it was. I counted 14 snowmobiles in various conditions in two neat rows on the shop floor. Some of them were on blocks and some of them were just sitting there. Most of them were small, but two were for average-size adults.

"Who drives the bigger ones?" I asked.

"Santa drives that one," Benny said, pointing to a red one painted with Christmas stars and Christmas trees, "and the other one is for Mrs. Claus. That's the one we'll take out this afternoon. She likes to ride it but she's not that into driving it, so it is set up for me to drive it and her to just ride along. I can reach all the controls in it."

"Cool!" I said. Mrs. Claus's snowmobile was green and it was painted with red-and-white candy canes.

"Do you have a favorite one to race?" I asked.

"Oh, I don't know; probably that one," Benny said, pointing to a small, bright blue snowmobile that had the number 24 in big white letters.

"It's pretty. You know, both your snowmobile and you remind me of one of my favorite sprint car drivers," I said.

"Why's that?"

"Well, one of my favorite drivers is named Rico," I explained. "He's number 24 too. And like you he's a great driver, he's very nice, and he's a little person too."

"You don't say?"

"Yes; and he always encourages people to follow their dreams. He says if you work hard you can do anything."

"That's true!"

"Yes, and he has a cool dog too; his dog's name is Gus."

Benny just chuckled.

"I have to do a little prep work before we go," he said. "You can look around the shop while you wait. It won't take me long."

There was a lot to look at. There were many big photos on the walls of Benny posing by different snowmobiles with trophies in victory lane ceremonies. In some of them he was holding big cardboard checks, and those same checks were on the walls too. There were so many trophies they lined shelves on one whole wall, and more spilled over onto the tops of filing cabinets, a desk, and a few cabinets.

"Wow Benny; you're really good!" I said, impressed.

"I've been driving snowmobiles since I was a kid," Benny said modestly.

"How old are you now?"

"I'll be 427 in July."

"Wow," I said again.

We continued to chat as Benny checked over Mrs. Claus's snowmobile.

"Miss Emma, I wanted to ask you something," he said. "What was it that made you aware of the problems of climate change?"

I settled onto a folding chair beside one of the filing cabinets.

"We talked about it in science class. My teacher, Mrs. Morgan, explained that it was a very serious problem."

"And what made you want to try to write about it?"

"Well, I like to write, and Mrs. Morgan says I'm good at it for my age. She says I have, what was the word? Potential. That's the first reason," I said.

"And after what Mrs. Morgan said about the environment, it seemed like something that people should know more about. Maybe if they understood what is at stake, they would do more to fix things. Books can help spread the word and get people to do things. That's the second reason."

"Sometimes grassroots efforts are the most effective," Benny agreed.

"The third reason is I thought maybe writing is something that I could get good at if I tried hard enough," I added. "I don't know what I want to be when I grow up exactly, but people are asking me about it already. I think it might be something involving writing, but I'm not sure. So I wanted to see if maybe I could do it."

"You're at the age that you should explore different things," Benny answered. "Lots of people don't know what they want to do even after they complete high school or college."

"Yeah," I agreed. "And the fourth reason is that Sophia and I are really worried about the environment — Sophia is my best friend," I continued, trying to explain. "She lives in an apartment complex, and her mom and dad don't have a car. She gets really worried when she sees pictures on the news of people leaving areas where there is a natural disaster like a hurricane or a fire or a flood. On the news there are lots of traffic jams of people leaving in their cars. Sophia's family always takes the bus. But the buses don't run when there are problems, and you can't take lots of things with you on a bus. So how will they get out?"

Benny looked serious. "Maybe they have family or friends in the area who have cars that they could go with? If they stay, the first responders will help them, or the Red Cross will set up a shelter where they can stay and be safe," he said. "But yes, it's all very worrisome. And natural disasters are going to increase since everything is so interrelated."

We were both quiet for a while.

"I think we're ready now," Benny said shortly. "You'll find snowmobile suits, helmets, gloves, and boots in all sizes in the room next to us; just go into the hall and then take the first door on the left."

Everything was well organized in the dressing room, and I quickly found a suit and other gear that would work, put it all on, and reported back to Benny. When I arrived he was already dressed too.

"OK; just sit back here," he said, pointing to the end of the snowmobile's seat, "and you can hold on to the edges of the seat or onto me. I won't go fast until you get the feel of it."

I climbed aboard, Benny pushed a button on the wall to open the garage door, and then he climbed aboard too. He spent a few minutes idling; I think it was just to warm the engine up. Once we were outside he stopped, got off the snowmobile to hit a button on the outside of the shop to close the garage door, climbed back onboard, and we were off!

It was fun! Even through my visor the crisp air struck my face as we navigated the curves and flew across the straight areas of snow. It was cold, but I discovered my seat was heated, which helped. I relaxed and just let my body sway with the movement of the snowmobile. All my worries about the environment and deadlines slipped to the back of my brain.

We hadn't gone far when Benny stopped and looked back at me.

"How are you doing? Do you need anything? Do you have any questions?" he asked.

"I'm fine! This is fun!"

As we zipped along it felt like we were one with nature; the feeling of freedom must be like what an eagle feels when it soars through the sky. Although our snowmobile was a little loud, it didn't seem to bother the pack of arctic foxes we saw to our left, or the herd of muskox to our right. Benny spotted them first, and pointed them out. I had never seen a muskox before, but I knew that's what they were because of their long, curved horns.

A little later Benny slowed down and spoke to me again. "We're going to head over by the shore. I want to check on something."

I had no idea what we were going to check on, but I couldn't wait to find out!

Belugas

It seemed like we were headed more to the mountains than the shore, as the snowmobile definitely was going uphill as we zipped along. The ice that had been hitting me now and then picked up, so I buried my face in the back of Benny's snowmobile suit and just hung on.

About 20 minutes later we stopped. When I looked up, an amazing view spread out in front of me. We were on a mountain, and the sea was below us. Glaciers rose up in front of us, behind the water, and little icebergs dotted the sea's surface. Although the sky had been like twilight so far during my trip, for some reason here it was a brilliant blue. It was very quiet, sort of like church before a service starts. As we watched, spellbound, water vapor periodically pierced the water's surface, and then the large head of a beluga whale poked out.

"They're here! Great!" Benny said aloud. "Hold on, we're going to get closer."

In a few minutes we were at the water's edge. Benny turned off the snowmobile's engine and we watched and listened. We were rewarded with the sight of a beluga rising up over the edge of the surface of the sea, continually making chirping and whistling noises as it communicated to the other belugas under the water.

"How beautiful!" I breathed.

"Yes," Benny agreed. "I'm glad to see them. I think there are about 10 in this pod. Less sea ice and warmer temperatures are attracting more cruise ships and larger boats to this area, which has been scaring off the whales. We get belugas like these, narwhals, and even orcas. They're all really sensitive to underwater noise. It screws up the way they find food, navigate, and communicate underwater. If they can't hear their clicks due to underwater noises caused by ships or underwater mining, they not only can't communicate with each other, but they can get disoriented and not know where they are."

Benny knew a lot about whales. "Lots of people don't know this, but about 20,000 whales are killed each year by ships," he continued. "Lots more are injured by them. Big ships like cruise ships are going faster than they used to, and they can't turn on a dime."

"It's just another bad thing we humans are doing to nature," I said sadly.

"Yes. People are supposed to be smarter than animals, but it often doesn't seem like they are," Benny said.

"I'm glad to see this group," he continued. "With climate change their food is moving, so the whales are moving too."

"What do they eat?"

"All sorts of things, but I think these particular belugas are going after cod."

We continued to watch the belugas occasionally pierce the water's surface with their tall and wide foreheads. Before they surfaced they looked like small pieces of ice floating in the sea. They were clicking away, talking to each other. It was almost like they were playing tag.

"There are things we could do that would help," Benny said a bit later. "Just slowing the speeds of the ships down would be one thing. Insisting on quieter engines would help too, because sounds travel four times faster in water than they do in air. Propellers and hulls could be designed better. Routes could be changed when we know a lot of whales are in the area. But it would take a lot of countries and companies getting together to make those changes stick around the world.

"Belugas are among the most social animals there are," he

added. "Narwhals are cool because of their tusks; blue whales are cool just because of their size, and orcas are great hunters, but I like belugas the best."

"I love all whales," I agreed. "Thank you so much for showing them to me!"

"I better get you home now," Benny answered, and we put our visors down and headed back to Grandma Hazel and the guest house. I felt sure this afternoon was something I'd remember all my life.

Donna

The next morning Grandma Hazel and I went looking for Donna.

"Isn't her name Donner?" I asked.

"She had it legally changed from Donner to Donna in 1878 when the amendment allowing women to vote in America was introduced to Congress," Grandma Hazel said. "She used it even before that though, as her stage name. You'll see."

Benny told us we would find Donna in the recital hall in the kingdom's main theater. When we entered, she was singing do-re-mi scales accompanied by a pianist. The pianist was a lady elf wearing a lavender dress, black thigh-high boots, and yellow plastic glasses.

Thigh-high boots aren't very high when they're worn by an elf.

Grandma Hazel and I sat in the plush red theater seats to watch and listen.

Donna wore a white pullover sweater and black leggings, and she had a lot of silver bangle bracelets around all four of her legs. She had black, oval-shaped metal glasses. A small rainbow pin was attached to her ruff with a red ribbon.

She had a black beret on her head. It must have been held on by bobby pins because it stayed on even when she swung her head and her antlers up and down to the scales. She had headphones on too. A microphone stood in front of her. A circular thing resembling an embroidery hoop with a screen on it stood in front of the microphone. A black music stand was beside the microphone, illuminated by a black desk light clipped to it.

She ran through a couple more scales before she saw us and nodded.

"Let's take 30, Arden," Donna said to the elf, who nodded, smiled at us, collected her music, slipped off the piano bench, and disappeared.

"I'm sorry, Donna. We're a little early," Grandma Hazel said.

"That's no problem," Donna said, smiling back at us. "I'll be right there."

"Ernie, we need to take 30 now," she said into the microphone, and then moved toward us. "Shall we go into the lounge?" she asked Grandma Hazel and me, pointing down a hall with her antlers.

The lounge was decorated for Christmas even though it was March. It had a piano too, and fifties-style bright red and green vinyl seats with chrome trim.

"So, Emma, right?" she asked me. "I understand you're from the United States. Do you live anywhere near New York City or Hollywood?"

"No, I live in the middle of the country," I said.

"That's a shame," Donna replied. "I adore New York and Los Angeles."

"Donna is one of the North Pole's brightest theatrical talents," Grandma Hazel said. "She often stars in our plays, and usually has solos in our concerts."

"You're very kind," Donna said.

I got out my notebook and pen. "I can already see what you do when you're not pulling Santa's sleigh. Please tell me more about yourself."

"Well, yes, I love to sing and act," Donna replied. "Rehearsals, performances, and appearances keep me busy. But when I do have time to relax, I just like to be at home since I travel so much.

"I do go skiing quite often, and I enjoy being by the fire at the ski lodges. One nice thing about the North Pole is there are no paparazzi up here!"

I tried to imagine the mechanics of reindeer skiing, but Donna was already pushing ahead.

"I understand you're writing a book to try to help our situation," she said. "I hope it's a smashing success! Maybe it will be made into a play or a movie, and I will finally get my Tony or Oscar! I would so love to be on Broadway or in Hollywood!"

"It's not even written yet," I reminded her. "It's going to be hard to write, too."

"You can do it if you try!" she said. "Good lyrics and a good script are so important! Just keep trying; the show must go on!"

"Thank you." I wondered how I was going to get all of this down. "Do you have a conservation tip for me?"

"Yes!" Donna took center stage in the lounge and paused before she spoke to make her answer more dramatic. "My tip is to drive less, use energy-friendly cars when you do drive, and service them regularly.

"And slow down and speed up gradually!," she said, getting excited. "Don't do jack-rabbit starts and stops!"

She regained her composure and continued in a very measured way. "Walk, bike, carpool, or take mass transit more often. That will help a lot. Carbon dioxide, a byproduct of fossil fuel combustion, is the principal greenhouse gas contributing to global warming.

"That's why I'm supportive of electric cars," she said. "Their batteries are getting better for longer driving time, car manufacturers are trying to make them more affordable, and they're the wave of the future."

"My dad makes fun of electric cars," I blurted out. "He doesn't think they're the answer. He says they don't go far enough on a charge, take too much fossil fuel to make, catch fire a lot, and use electricity from power plants that still use fossil fuels."

I'm not sure what got into me, but more rolled out. "He says their old batteries will be in our landfills forever. He also says electric cars break down a lot. They get terrible tire wear too. He thinks the whole electric vehicle movement is a ploy for millionaires to make even more money."

Donna looked at me. I could hear the seconds tick by on a clock hanging on the wall. I couldn't believe I had voiced a difference of opinion to a reindeer star. I wondered if she'd even give me a tip for my book now.

"Is your father a scientist or an engineer?"

"No. He sells insurance."

"Humpf," she replied. A few more seconds passed.

"Yes, much more work needs to be done, but the brightest minds in the world are working on answers to these problems," she said evenly. "It's a huge challenge, and it won't be fixed overnight.

"If you must drive, there are still things you can do to help," she continued. "I regularly remind my chauffeur, Jules, to check my limo's tires. Keeping tires inflated properly can help you improve your gas mileage by more than 3 percent!"

I wrote it all down.

"Another thing is that politics always play a role in entertainment and government," Donna added. "No matter how successful an actor is, he or she often has to convince a director to cast them in a role. The same thing is true in politics. Kids and their parents have to convince their representatives in government that conservation is important and should be a top priority. That's called lobbying. You need to write letters to your leaders, call them, send emails, and conduct polls to convince them they need to work on the environment immediately. You can tell them that you won't ever vote for them again if they don't. They'll get the idea," she concluded.

Soon it was time to go. But before we left, I got her autograph in my notebook.

The Bear

When we left the theater, Grandma Hazel said she had to stop by her pharmacy to pick up a prescription. She said I could go with her or take a shortcut over a small glacier behind the theater and beat her back to the guest house.

I opted to go ahead. The snow crunched under my boots and my eyes watered from the cold, but I was warm enough as I walked along.

While I walked, I got an uneasy feeling that something was watching me. I shrugged it off and kept going.

And then, somewhere behind me, I heard a growl.

I turned. A huge polar bear loomed about 15 feet behind me.

Polar bears might be on the list for extinction, but this one was definitely right here, right now. And he looked ravenous.

I had no idea what to do. Should I run? Should I stay still? Should I stop and raise my arms and try to scare him off? I wished I could Google the answer!

I kept walking at the same pace and hoped the bear would go away.

He didn't.

He sped up and got closer. I could see his short, very black, and very sharp claws as they dug into the ice. He opened his mouth to growl at me again, and I also saw his yellow, very sharp teeth. I knew that polar bears can bite the head off a seal in one bite, and this one could do the same to me!

Suddenly icy water streamed in front of me and on both sides of the ice I was walking on. I had no idea how deep it was, but I wouldn't survive long if I fell in. I was trapped at the front and both sides by water, and by the polar bear behind me.

I'm going to die right here, before I even turn 12. There probably won't be enough left of me to even bury me. Mom, Dad, and Jacob will never know what happened to me.

The bear sniffed the air and smacked his teeth together like he was getting ready to rush me and chomp down on my head.

Desperate, I looked around for something to hit him with, but nothing was available. Terror overtook me. I stared at the bear and hoped it would be over soon.

It was, but not in the way I feared.

I heard tiny bells, and suddenly Grandma Hazel appeared between me and the bear, and she squirted a can of bear spray right into his eyes!

The bear howled as the bear spray hit his eyes and his lungs. Grandma Hazel kept spraying until the can was empty and there was a cloud of spray between us and the bear. Finally he turned, dove into the water beside us with a big splash, and disappeared.

"Are you OK?" Grandma Hazel asked breathlessly.

"Now I am!" I whispered.

"Let's get you home," Grandma Hazel said. "We'll catch up with Blitzen tomorrow." She said something too low for me to hear, moved her arms in her unique way, and transported us back to my bedroom at the pink guest house without another word.

"You saved my life!" I said.

"It was scary," Grandma Hazel admitted. "My prescription wasn't ready yet, so I took the same shortcut you took and I wasn't far behind you. I had no idea that there was a break in that glacier.

"It's another example of global warming," she added. "That ice should have been stable. And that bear most likely would have avoided you if his stomach hadn't been empty because he can't get enough to eat due to climate change."

It was just another reason why I have to write the book.

Blitzen

The next morning we set out for my interview with the last reindeer, Blitzen.

"Frau Blitzen is German," Grandma Hazel said. "So is Santa. A lot of Christmas traditions come straight from Germany, even though Santa was born in Turkey."

Blitzen was punctual. She met us beside a Glühwein Pyramide at the Christkindlmarkt. The market was closed but there were still a few elf vendors around, preparing for the next market day. I could hear polka music playing in the distance as they worked.

The Pyramide itself was beautiful. The traditional German Christmas decoration was over 30 feet tall. It was made of pine and decorated with candles, wreaths, evergreen garlands, angels, and thousands of Christmas lights. Its six giant fan blades weren't revolving but they towered above us like a huge ceiling fan.

Blitzen seemed to be larger than a typical reindeer. A striking pendant hung on a thick blue cord around her neck and nestled in her ruff. The cord consisted of three strands of cording twisted together, and it had a big gold clasp. When I admired the pendant, she said it was a German coat of arms, and she wore it because it represented one of her favorite trees, the linden. Sapphires and emeralds flanked both sides of the artwork. I could tell it was expensive.

I could also tell that Blitzen was athletic by her muscles and her gestures. Grandma Hazel said she was the fastest reindeer on the team, and in German her name means "Flash." She said Blitzen was as fast as a bolt of lightning.

Considering that, I wondered if she minded being the last reindeer when she was hitched to Santa's sleigh. Blitzen set me straight.

"Not at all," she said. "Do you know the saying 'The first shall be last and the last shall be first,' or the one about 'Save the best for last?'"

"I've heard them both before," I said. "Mom always tells me another one, 'To finish first, first you must finish.'"

"That's a good one too," Blitzen said. "So is 'Things aren't always what they seem.' My position on the line has nothing to do with my speed. Santa wants me in that spot so I'm near to him in the sleigh. That way, should we run into a problem on Christmas Eve, we can discuss possible solutions quickly."

"Blitzen has saved the day several times," Grandma Hazel told me.

"And you're the fastest reindeer on the team?" I asked.

"I try."

"Is there any significance to you wanting to meet us here?" I asked.

Blitzen pawed at the snow and then pointed with her antlers to a small shop, which was nothing more than a shed. "Come this way."

Inside the shed, hundreds of colorful nutcracker soldiers lined shelves around its four walls, from top to bottom. They were of varying heights and colors, but all were beautiful. Some held swords or walking sticks. Most had beards, many made of small pieces of white fur. The shop smelled of wood shavings, but it was tidy.

"On my daily walks and runs, I look for tree branches we can use to carve nutcrackers," she said. "I bring them to the workshop, and our master woodcrafter elves carve them into these beautiful nutcrackers. Sometimes I help with the painting and decorating."

"They're beautiful," I said.

"We're proud of them," Blitzen said. "My team also makes cuckoo clocks from the wood I bring them."

"I bet they're pretty too," I said.

"I'm glad you enjoy them; they are old crafts," she said. "I love to pick up the wood that's fallen from the trees on my walks."

She looked at me closely. "I don't know if children your age even like to walk in the woods anymore," she added. "It seems like you only like to blow people up in video games."

"Kids still like to walk in the woods," I assured her.

Blitzen nodded. "I love wood and trees," she said. "Trees make the whole world nicer. I think trees are one of the most amazing things God ever created. They can be big or small. I'm partial to evergreens, but in other places in the world there are trees with colorful leaves in autumn that are also amazing. And I've seen beautiful pictures of cherry trees and dogwoods in the spring.

"Trees give us clean air to breathe," she continued. "They absorb carbon dioxide and produce oxygen. They filter out pollution, and their bark and leaves trap bad things in the air to help us breathe better. They provide fruit and nuts, and food for many species, like us reindeer. They give us shade and windbreaks and they help with drainage, which saves energy."

"And you can climb them," I chipped in. I thought about the chestnut trees in my backyard at home. I liked to climb one in particular, sit on a fork in its branches, and read.

"And you can build tree houses in them." Blitzen nodded. "They also prevent erosion because they have large roots to keep the soil in place."

"They give us lumber," Grandma Hazel pointed out.

"Yes; so many things are made of wood," Blitzen added. "People make houses out of trees, and they're home to many different animals.

"That's why I make it a point to plant as many trees as possible," she added. "Planting trees is one of my hobbies. A single tree will absorb one ton of carbon dioxide over its lifetime, so one of my tips is for the children to plant as many trees as possible.

"People could also eat less meat and take up gardening," she added. "If they grow their own fresh fruits and vegetables they would enjoy fresher food and we'd save the energy we're currently using to transport their produce. They would also find that gardening is fun. At the very least they could buy locally grown produce."

I tried to get it all down in my notebook.

"We must all work together," she concluded. "If we can save the environment, it will be the most important thing we will ever do."

Grandma Hazel was still standing nearby.

"Is the meeting with Isabella still on?" she asked Blitzen.

"I think so. She hates humans so much that I don't know if she'll show up, but we'll try."

I had no idea what they were talking about, but I was pretty sure I was the only human around.

"Emma, Blitzen would like you to meet a friend of hers," Grandma Hazel said. "She'll take you to meet her and then bring you back to the house. I'll go on ahead."

And with that, she disappeared.

I wondered who Isabella was and why she hated humans, including me.

Isabella

"Come," Blitzen directed. "It's a short walk to the end of this glacier."

We walked together silently for about 10 minutes, and then I could sense and smell water ahead. A few steps later there was nothing but the ocean before us in a thick fog, which made the land and the sea run together endlessly in a totally gray, gloomy world. There was no real sign of life; even the seabirds had disappeared.

My clothes were damp. I could smell the salt of the sea and the pungent odor of seaweed, and thanks to the fog I could even taste the salt in the air. It was twilight, just like it had mostly been since I arrived. But there was no sense of the anticipation of nightfall and stars. Everything was just cold and gray. The only sound was the waves lapping at the shore, but even they sounded tired and unhappy, as if they were being forced into motion by the moon against their will.

Blitzen lowered her head with its mighty antlers and looked at the water.

And we waited.

After a while, Blitzen sighed and looked at a German watch buckled around her left-front leg, near her hoof. "She might not come," she said. "She said she would try, but that I wasn't to count on it. We'll give her a few more minutes."

I didn't respond because my teeth were chattering from the cold. I shivered under my pink coat, and reached into my coat pocket for one of my last tissues to wipe my runny nose. I was wearing purple mittens, but I thrust my hands into my coat pockets to keep them warmer.

Suddenly there were a few tiny bubbles in the water in front of us. Milliseconds later, long whiskers appeared above the surface of the water. Then, in one big swoosh, a seal burst out of the water and onto the ice in front of us, on her belly.

But she was unlike any seal I'd ever seen at the zoo or any pictures of seals I'd ever seen in books or on TV.

She was small, about the size of a crow, and her skin was the color of lilacs. She had two purple wings on either side of her body. They looked more like the wings of a dragon than a bird though; the outsides looked like the rest of her seal skin. There weren't any feathers, but the membranes under her wings were a stunning display of every pastel color I'd ever seen. The colors all ran together and were streaked with gold. The closest thing I had ever seen to them was the opal ring Mom got as an inheritance from her Aunt Diane.

Although the wings were a big surprise, the most striking thing about her was her large eyes, which seemed too big for her body. They were dark purple, and they were bottomless. They also seemed terribly sad.

"Ah, Isabella, I'm so glad you came," Blitzen said, and then she talked to the seal in a series of funny barks, grunts, and whines.

"Isabella doesn't know English and you don't know Sealish, so I'll act as your interpreter," Blitzen told me.

"Please tell her 'Hello,' for me," I said. Blitzen proceeded to make funny noises, but Isabella seemed to understand.

"I'll save some time here and give you Isabella's background," Blitzen said, speaking directly to me. "Isabella is the last of the species chiroptera violaceous pinniped, an animal so rare that humans never discovered it."

"A chiroptera...?" My words trailed off. I took out my notebook, found my pen, took off my mittens to write, and wondered how to spell chiroptera.

"A chiroptera violaceous pinniped means a winged seal of a pale purple color," Blitzen said.

I gave up and asked something else. "OK. But how can she hear you if she doesn't have ears?"

"She can hear as well as you can; it's just that her ears aren't on the outside of her body," Blitzen replied. "And of course you noticed her wings."

"Yes." Even though it was freezing, I began writing in my notebook again. "I love the colors on the underside."

"Yes. The colors on the underside of her wings are unlike any other in the animal kingdom," Blitzen agreed. "Her species was the only seal to ever fly."

"Was?"

"Unfortunately, yes," Blitzen continued. "As far as we know, Isabella is the last of her species. Her parents and her brother died a few years ago, and her mate, Ethan, died a few months ago. All of them were victims of humans and their misuse of the environment."

I swallowed hard. "How old is she?"

"She's younger than you in human years, but she's a young adult in seal years," Blitzen said. "She was looking forward to becoming a mother. She and Ethan were very much in love."

"But they're all dead now?"

"Yes. Her father was killed by the propellers of an oil freighter that sailed right into their migratory path. Her mother died of lung cancer she got from breathing smog as they migrated past Los Angeles.

"Her brother, Liam, got caught in some plastic used to hold a six-pack of soda together. Someone carelessly threw it out into the water, he got entangled in it, and he drowned. Isabella tried to help him get free, but he died right in front of her."

"How awful!"

"And the love of her life, Ethan, died a hero's death," Blitzen said. "He used his wings to fly into the area of a California wildfire, which was larger and more intense due to global warming, to try to save other animals. The winds shifted, and he, a family of raccoons, and three rabbits that he was trying to lead to safety all died of smoke inhalation. One rabbit made it out alive and told Isabella what happened, but he died later too."

"That is horrible," I said. Isabella watched me carefully. "And there are no other seals like her on the whole Earth?"

"We don't think so," Blitzen said. "Isabella is the last one we know of. There is a rumor there might be a few of her kind at the South Pole, but it's too far for any of us to go to try to find them. I volunteered to fly Santa there, but he said we couldn't spare the magic lichen to make such a long trip.

"Our elf scientists and horticulturists are working together to try to produce magic lichen in our greenhouses, but everything they've come up with so far has been inedible," she continued. "When they tried it in pill form, not only did our reindeer not fly, it had a bad side effect and made them the other kind of jumpy. Their nerves were shot!"

"That's not good. And poor Isabella!" I said sadly, nodding my head sideways. "And that's why she hates people?"

"Yes." Blitzen made some whiney noises and grunts which Isabella understood. She glared at me, which made me squirm.

"So that brings us to this impasse," Blitzen said. "Isabella wants to know why your species is so arrogant that it can destroy entire species of other animals and not care enough to even try to do anything about it. Humans over-populate the world. Isn't there even a tiny spot on the planet where winged lilac seals can live in peace? She wants to know what seals ever did to you. She doesn't know what makes people think they are better than any other animal.

"And she is furious that some humans are so stupid that they say climate change is not real," Blitzen continued. "Scientists agree it's real and humans are the cause, but many people don't believe them. And some people say global warming is all due to natural factors, but that's not the cause. It's caused by the billions of tons of carbon pollution people create. The pollution causes water to evaporate from land faster, making heat waves, droughts, floods, and wildfires more frequent and intense. It plays havoc with the water supply, and kills plants and many other things.

"Our polar ice is connected to the weather patterns that reach across the world," she continued. "As the ice melts, more extreme weather occurs, which fuels wildfires. Sea levels rise, which causes floods. It's all connected!"

Isabella might not have understood Blitzen's words, but she seemed to sense their meaning. She growled and looked at me accusingly.

"I didn't do it," I pointed out softly.

"No, you humans never take responsibility," Blitzen said, not waiting for Isabella's input. "As a species, humans do terrible things, but you pass the blame to each other and tell yourselves it's too big of a problem for you to solve individually. You are all to blame, and you continue to do things that make it worse, because to you, it's never your fault."

Blitzen wasn't finished.

"Isabella wants you to think about what it would be like if you were in her situation. What if you had lost everyone who mattered to you? What if you always wanted to be a mother, and now you will never be one naturally, there is no one to adopt, and you have no future? She says no one can understand how sad and lonely she is. She says she might as well die now instead of prolonging her grief."

I looked into Isabella's dark eyes and wiped an icy tear off my cheek.

"I'm so sorry," I said, but even as I said it I knew words were not enough.

This Is Hard

The next morning, right after another one of Grandma Hazel's great breakfasts, I was determined to start writing my book to tell everyone we must fix things NOW.

There was no computer in my bedroom, but I pulled my notebook out from the new briefcase Mr. Strauss had given me and opened it up on the top of the desk. Then I got out all my colorful pens and lined them up beside my notebook.

I hadn't made my bed yet, so I stopped to do that first. Then I remembered I hadn't put my dirty clothes in the hamper down the hall like Grandma Hazel had asked me to do, so I took care of that too.

The alarm clock on my bedside table said 9:10 a.m.

I decided to start writing at 9:30. That way I'd know exactly how many hours I spent writing today.

Since I had 20 minutes, I sat in the window seat and looked down at the street below. It had snowed last night, and two elves were shoveling the sidewalk across the street. They were working quickly and their mouths were moving like they were singing, but I couldn't hear the words to their song.

I watched them for a while, and since I wanted to know what song they were singing, I opened the window a little to hear better.

It was "Jingle Bells."

After a while it got too cold to have the window open, so I closed it. I looked at the alarm clock again. It was 9:34, so I returned to my desk to review my notes.

In my excitement from meeting the reindeer, I had skipped around in my notebook while I took notes. I couldn't read some of them, and others were all mixed up. I got out my brightest red pen and tried to put the pages in chronological order. I wrote the page number in red in the top-right corner of each page and drew a circle around it.

There were a lot of pages, and it was confusing. I thought it might help to see everything at once, so I tore all the pages out, put them on the floor, and began to arrange them there.

It was a lot of work, and after being stooped over for so long the room spun a little.

How can I organize this information into something kids would want to read?

I thought it might go more smoothly after I took a break, so I rearranged the clothes in my closet by color. That took quite a long time because there were a lot of clothes and this was the first time anyone had ever put them in order.

While I was doing that, I wondered why Grandma Hazel was so sure I could write a book. I hadn't been able to finish the one on global warming, and this book was going to be quite a bit more complicated.

There were other kids in my class at school who wrote just as well or maybe even better than I did, like Alexandra Heller. She wrote a Halloween story about some monsters. Our teacher read it aloud in class, and I think it was better than anything I could ever write.

A not-so-nice voice in my head spoke up then, and it was so loud I couldn't help hearing it. It said no book I would ever write would be good enough to be published, let alone be good enough to convince children around the world to change their bad habits and think about conservation and the Earth more.

The more I thought about it, the more I thought that voice was probably right. After all, I didn't have much of that "gumption" Santa talked about.

Why did Grandma Hazel even bring me here? Doesn't she know I'm too young to write a book, and I have trouble finishing things?

How did I ever get roped into trying to do this? I'm not that good.

Eventually I got tired of rearranging the clothes in my closet. I was arranging them according to the colors of the rainbow: red, orange, yellow, green, blue, indigo, and violet. The first letter of each color spells the name Roy G. Biv. We learned that last year in science class. I was up to green, but my arms were tired now, so I lay back down on the bed.

Thinking about the rainbow made me wonder why Grandma Hazel hadn't answered my question about our family being related to the leprechauns who guard the pots of gold at the end of rainbows.

I think I need to ask her again.

I must have fallen asleep because the next thing I knew Grandma Hazel was knocking on my door telling me it was time for lunch.

We had extra-cheesy pizza, my favorite!

I volunteered to do the dishes after lunch.

When I got back to my room it was 1:19 p.m. I decided to start working on the book again at 1:30. Since that was only 11 minutes from now, I didn't have much time. I went to the bathroom and brushed my teeth, since you should always brush your teeth after a meal, especially if that meal includes cheese that sticks to your teeth and if you have braces like I do.

I looked at my notes, still lying on the floor. I moved some of them around until the order was pretty close. I was almost finished putting the numbers in the circles on every page when my red pen ran out of ink. I looked in the desk drawer for another red pen. I couldn't find one, even though I knew I had one. I sighed and finished doing the numbering with a green pen. At least it was Christmassy.

Then I picked up all the pages from the floor in order and took them back to the desk.

I looked for bubblegum but couldn't find any in the desk

drawer. I thought about going to the store to get some, but I didn't want to ask Grandma Hazel for any money.

My nose started to run a bit. I guess that's to be expected when you're at the North Pole, where it's always cold. I went to the bathroom and found some tissues. I used some and then brought the box back to my desk.

My first page of notes looked up at me, right where I'd left it. I picked it up and tried to read my handwriting. It was pretty messy, but I figured most of it out.

I tore out a fresh piece of notepaper to use for the start of my book. I tried not to think about how hard it was going to be to write a whole book.

How many pages are in a whole book, anyway? It's too bad all my books are back home in my real bedroom, where I can't refer to them.

I looked at my first page of notes again. Nothing came to me, so I tried reading the notes aloud.

Again, nothing.

I looked at the fresh piece of notepaper on my desk, so clean and optimistic that someone would put some wonderful words on it.

I had no idea how to start.

I moved my right leg up and down and then side to side so I wouldn't get a cramp.

I thought hard about the best way to begin, but I was still drawing a blank.

Even though I knew I shouldn't, I climbed up on the bed and jumped on the mattress for a while. Mom would have been on me as fast as Santa's reindeer fly, but Grandma Hazel either didn't hear me or didn't want to tell me to stop.

I thought about what would happen if I couldn't finish this book that I couldn't even start right now.

The reindeer will be so disappointed! So will Santa! And how sad Grandma Hazel will be after she showed so much confidence in me!

And what about all the good tips the reindeer gave me to tell the kids what to do to stop global warming and save the world? If I can't write this book, all those wonderful animals and plants will become extinct, and it will all be my fault. Well, not all my fault, but mostly so.

And what about Isabella?

I put my head down on my desk. I drew some doodles on a fresh piece of paper until some tears dropped on them and made them go fuzzy. And then I guess I cried myself to sleep.

A Walk Might Help

The next morning Grandma Hazel asked me how the writing was going.

"Terrible," I said. "It is a complicated subject. I don't even know how to start."

"Perhaps it would help if you try to break the work down into more manageable pieces, rather than thinking about the whole project at once," she suggested. "Maybe if you try to make an outline, a way to organize it will appear. You could start by going over all the reindeer's tips."

"I'll try that," I said, but deep inside I was doubtful.

When I returned to my desk, I looked at my pile of notes.

I thought about Grandma Hazel's advice, but there were so many layers to this story. I grabbed a pen and wrote them down. I should write about how interesting each reindeer is. I should include meeting Santa and what he said about having gumption, breaking bad habits, and the importance of teamwork. I should stress each reindeer's tips on ways to save the planet from global warming. And of course I should write about Isabella. And somehow I should convince each kid who reads the book that time is running out and we need to act now or there will be no more Christmases, more plants and animals will go extinct, and we'll have more natural disasters.

I had to get it all in, and yet not be bossy about it. I certainly didn't want to be like the bossiest girl in my class, Gloria Picardy. Gloria was bossy and snooty to boot.

I thought about what would happen if I couldn't get it all down, and if I couldn't make it into something kids would want to read.

I thought about how some scientists would probably point out things I should have said but didn't, or things I didn't get quite right.

I gulped, but the dryness of my mouth wouldn't go away.

I put that sheet of paper aside, went through my notes, and copied each reindeer's conservation tips.

That took the rest of the morning.

That afternoon I tried again. I thought about starting with Santa since he's a bigger "star" than the reindeer. I tried beginning with his explanation about how to break a bad habit, but I couldn't figure out why he would be talking about that first before I explained why we needed to break our bad habits.

I thought maybe an idea would come if I just started to write.

"I don't know what to write," I wrote. Then I wrote that sentence again.

Under that I put "By Emma Gallagher." But that made me scared, since I'm not really an author.

What business do I have telling people what they should and shouldn't do? I have no research behind me. I just have tips from some animals. And who is going to believe reindeer can talk?

I looked out the window at the street below. Snowflakes played tag with each other as they tumbled by the window pane.

"Maybe if I take a walk, I'll be able to think more clearly and get some gumption," I thought.

My coat and boots were right where I'd left them, but finding my hat and mittens took me a while. I put them on and went downstairs. Grandma Hazel snoozed in her recliner. A Christmas book lay upside down on her lap, and she emitted a soft snore now and then.

I won't be gone long.

I brought my notes and a pen in the briefcase Mr. Strauss had given me, just in case I got inspired and needed to write something down quickly, before I forgot it.

It was colder than I thought it would be, but the fresh air felt crisp and clean on my face. My breath made water vapor. The Northern Lights flashed their wisps of green, purple, and yellow above the horizon, like they were taunting me to come closer.

I walked past the reindeer barn, climbed over a fence, and trudged out into the open field where they have races, flight school, and play reindeer games. Cupid's archery targets were covered in snow.

It was hard going because there wasn't a path. I felt sure my cheeks were red. My nose was running too, but I kept going. It would be good to accomplish something, even if it was just getting a little exercise.

The reindeer barn grew tiny behind me. I aimed for the mountain ahead of me and kept taking slow steps through the snow.

The wind was picking up. Even though the sun wasn't out, my skin was getting red like I was getting a sunburn. My teeth started to chatter too.

The snow stung as it hit my face. I was surprised it was snowing this hard. I hadn't read the weather forecast in "The North Pole Times."

I smacked my lips to try to make the dryness go away.

Why am I so thirsty?

The snow beneath my feet became more icy and slippery, and I almost lost my balance a couple of times. It was sort of like walking on a frozen lake.

I was about to turn around when a gust of wind tore my briefcase out of my hands. I realized with horror that both it and my notes were gone.

Suddenly I lost my balance and fell into a deep opening in the ice. A sharp pain pierced through me as I heard a bone in my right arm crack.

Then everything in this entirely white world went black.

I'm Found, But All Is Lost

When I woke up I was in a metal bed at North Pole General Hospital.

My right arm was in a cast. A long red bandage looped over sections of it to make it look like a candy cane. The bandage was made out of wrinkly material that stuck to itself and looked like crepe paper.

All the clothes I had on before my walk were gone. I was wearing a hospital gown with pictures of little green gift boxes with red bows all over it.

There were three thick, warm blankets over me. The smell of the wool in the blankets mixed with the antiseptic aroma of the hospital room.

I found out later they were treating me for hypothermia because my body was too cold. A solution of warm salt water dripped into a needle at the top of my left hand. It was coming from a plastic bag on a pole beside my bed. A face mask attached to tubing covered my face. Humidified oxygen flowed through the tubing to help raise the temperature of my body.

I was a mess.

I was a little scared at first, but then I saw Grandma Hazel sleeping in a chair on the right side of my bed. Santa was in another chair on the left side of my bed, but he was wide awake.

"Well, good morning Emma!" he said cheerfully but softly so as not to wake Grandma Hazel, who snored lightly.

I moved the face mask aside with my good hand. "Good morning," I whispered to Santa. "Did you stay awake all night?"

"Well, the part of the song that says 'He sees you when you're sleeping, he knows when you're awake' is true," Santa said, and he winked at me.

I smiled. Then I sneezed loudly, waking Grandma Hazel up.

"Emma, dear, how do you feel?" she asked.

"I'm fine, I think," I said. "What happened to me?"

"You fell into a hole when a glacier split open, and you broke your arm and suffered hypothermia," Grandma Hazel told me. "You might have suffered a slight concussion too. Your vital signs are good now though."

"Who found me?" I asked.

"First, you should have never left without telling me where you were going," Grandma Hazel scolded. "You're lucky this story didn't end tragically."

"I'm sorry."

Santa continued to clue me in. "Benny saw you walking behind the reindeer barn but didn't think anything of it," he said. "But when you weren't home for supper, Grandma Hazel sounded the alarm.

"Benny told us the direction you were walking, but we had no way of knowing where you were since the storm broke about that time," Santa continued. "There was a whiteout, where no one could see a thing."

Grandma Hazel picked it up from there. "Do you remember when Dancer told you reindeer can see ultraviolet light better than other animals? They can even see white things in the snow. That's what saved you."

Santa elaborated. "We searched for you until we found you," he said. "I was just going to hitch up two reindeer to the sleigh to save time since we didn't have a big load of toys, but the team wouldn't hear of it. All eight insisted on going to look for you."

That made me happy.

"Benny went too since he knew the general direction you were headed," Santa continued. "That proved to be a lucky break. After the team spotted you down in that hole, I tied a rope to the runners of the sleigh and threw the rope down the hole. Benny was small enough to be able to climb down the rope. He tied the end of it around your waist, held on tight, and the team pulled both of you out, slick as could be!"

I could tell Santa was proud of them. I was proud too, and grateful.

"Do you mean to tell me I got to ride in your sleigh, and I slept through the whole thing?" I asked him.

"You were out like a light," Santa replied.

"Just my luck." I tugged at the top blanket. "I'm getting a little hot."

"That's a good sign," Grandma Hazel said. Santa pulled the top blanket off me.

"Emma, when you are discharged tomorrow, I want Grandma Hazel to take you home," Santa told us both.

"But I don't have the book even started," I said. Then something occurred to me. "I don't know how I'm going to write it now either, since I'm right-handed and my right arm is broken.

"Oh! And I lost all my notes!" I remembered with a thud in my heart.

"After Grandma Hazel beams you back to your bedroom, you'll be in the same condition you were before your visit," Santa said. "Your arm will be fine; you won't have a cast. I don't want to have to explain to the authorities or your parents how you got hurt."

"But what about the book?" I said.

"I'm afraid there won't be a book," Santa said. "It was a difficult assignment for a kid from the start."

I'm glad he was understanding, but I felt like a failure.

"What will the reindeer say?" I said, tears sliding down my cheeks. "I let the team down. I let you and Grandma Hazel down.

I let Isabella down. There won't be any more magic lichen, and so eventually there won't be any more Christmases. The kids won't get the message to change their bad habits and save the planet. Plants and animals are going to go extinct because of me."

"Here, child, it's not your fault," Grandma Hazel said. "You tried; it was just too hard for you at this age."

"Can't I stay and try harder?" I asked Santa. "Maybe if I try again, I'll get some gumption and be able to finish what I started."

"No, you're going home in the morning," Santa insisted. "I have a responsibility to your parents. It's just too dangerous. We have traveled over that glacier for centuries without a problem. The fact that it cracked is unheard of. I'm afraid it's just another example of the changes occurring due to global warming.

"I'll check in on you at your house this coming Christmas Eve," he continued. "The important thing is you return to your parents in one piece. Now try to get some rest. Grandma Hazel will beam you home in the morning."

Back Home Again

Part of me wanted to see the reindeer before I left, but another part didn't want to since I had let them down.

That second part won. I just couldn't face them.

Grandma Hazel came to the hospital in the morning, signed my discharge papers, and we went back to the guest house.

Benny was waiting for us outside the house on a tiny silver snowmobile.

"I just wanted to check on you, Miss Emma," he said.

"I'm fine, Benny, and thank you for helping to rescue me. Please tell the reindeer I said thank you to them too."

"We're all just glad you're OK," he said. "It was a pleasure to meet you, and I hope you enjoyed your stay."

"I really did, Benny. I loved getting to know all of you and learning everything you taught me. I'm sorry I won't be able to write the book."

"Ah, it's just one of those things," Benny said, shrugging. "You take good care, and continue to be a good girl!" he added, and then he buckled his red helmet and zipped away.

Grandma Hazel and I went inside.

I went upstairs to take one last look at the lovely bedroom I had stayed in and then went downstairs and told her I was ready to go home.

"I'll miss you, Grandma Hazel," I said, hugging her so tightly I could smell her spicy perfume. "I love you."

"I love you too, child," she said, hugging me just as tightly. "I'm so glad I got to meet you and spend at least a little bit of time with you."

With that, it was time to go. We beamed down and flew past the beautiful green, pink, and purple lights. We rocketed along the stars and suddenly I was back in my own bedroom.

Pansy was still on my bed. My alarm clock still said 7:57 p.m. My arm wasn't in a cast, my headache was gone, and I was wearing jeans and my blue sweatshirt with the pink bunny on the front.

"Pansy, did you miss me?" I asked her. She stretched her spine toward the ceiling, circled the spot she had been lying on, and lay down again.

"To her, you never left," Grandma Hazel said. "Remember, time stood still for the ones we left behind."

Grandma Hazel sighed. "I hate goodbyes, so I'll just say see you later," she whispered. "But I'll also tell you something I hope you'll remember: 'You can do anything if you put your mind to it.'"

And then she was gone.

* * * *

Grandma Hazel was right; it was like I had never left home. I got up in the morning, ate breakfast, got ready for school, and had another typical boring day in the life of Emma Gallagher.

At first it was hard not to tell anyone about my adventure, especially my friend Sophia. I really wanted to tell her all about it. But since I had already let everyone at the North Pole down because I didn't write the book, I was determined not to let them down on something else, and I didn't say a word about it to anyone. I would keep their secret, even if I couldn't stop thinking about elves, reindeer, and a purple seal with wings.

As time passed I found I was making small changes in my daily life. I remembered to turn off the water when brushing my teeth instead of letting it run the entire time. I suggested to my mom that she and the other moms in our neighborhood set up a carpool for our soccer practices, so they wouldn't have to drive all of us kids there each time in separate cars. I also asked my dad if we could switch any of our remaining incandescent lightbulbs to LEDs when I saw they were on sale in an ad that came to the house. And Sophia and I made our science fair project about composting. We won second prize.

I kept thinking about that unfinished book and wished I had my notes.

* * * *

Finally school was out for the summer!

I got up early on the first day of summer vacation, sat at the desk in my bedroom, and looked at the piece of notebook paper and the pen in front of me. Without my notes, I only had what was in my head and heart.

I still didn't know how to start.

Do you know you can write almost all the letters of the alphabet in one long line without lifting your pen? The only letter that doesn't come out right is "F" because it looks too much like "E." "S" and "T" are a little off too.

I decided to start with Santa since everyone knows him.

I spent more than a week on that first version, but as it went on everything got muddled up. I had to go back and forth so much to explain things, even I got mixed up.

Deep down I knew it was awful, so I threw it in the trash. But then I remembered it was paper and I should recycle it, so I fished it out of the waste can and put all that hard work in the recycling bin in the garage.

Tree Hugger

The old me would have just quit there, but I wanted to prove to Santa — and myself — that I had gumption. So the next morning I got another notebook out and tried again. This notebook was pink and purple — my favorite colors. Maybe that would bring me some good luck.

I have a small smart TV in my bedroom, and after some surfing I found a YouTube video of "The Grand Old Opry Stars Sing Your Christmas Favorites." I hit "play." I didn't know most of the singers but I knew all the songs, and I think it helped.

I lay on my bed on my stomach with the notebook and my pen in front of me, thinking about how to start.

I thought about everything I wanted to say, which just made me nervous. When I remembered I didn't have any notes, it made me even more nervous.

I thought about everything I had learned and everyone I had met at the North Pole. I asked myself which person or animal had made the biggest impression on me. That was easy — Isabella.

So I started to tell Isabella's story. I tried to write about what it would be like to be her. I thought about how sad it would be to have no family left. What would it be like if there was no one left on Earth who looked like you, talked like you, or had the same problems as you?

It was all so lonely and sad.

Since I didn't know what the ending to Isabella's story would be, my story sort of spun around without going anywhere.

I worked on it for a whole week before it joined my first attempt in the recycling bin.

* * * *

A few mornings after that I tried again, but hours later I was no closer to having anything remotely good. I glared at the notebook in front of me, rolled my head in a circle to ease my stiff muscles, and rubbed the back of my neck.

I re-read the last page through hardened eyes, sighed, and clenched my jaw.

I read it again while absent-mindedly tapping the clicker of my favorite pen on my desk up and down. I tapped the pen so hard it flew apart. The spring rolled under my desk, and black ink smeared onto my fingers and the notebook.

I searched for a tissue, but of course I couldn't find the box I knew was somewhere in my bedroom. I slammed the notebook closed, marched to the bathroom, and tried to get the ink off my hands with water that was way too hot.

"Emma! Lunch!" I heard my mom yell.

My brother, Jacob, was already at the table when I stomped into the room.

"How's it going, Tree Hugger?" he asked.

I tried to ignore him like I do with most of the things concerning my brother, but I lost it.

"You are such a goon!" I yelled. "You are part of the problem! You think you can do whatever you want, with no consequences! Well, there are big consequences! There is only one Earth, you know!"

"Tree hugger! Tree hugger! Tree hugger!" Jacob chanted in response.

"Kids! Cut it out!" Mom warned.

I just wanted Jacob to shut up. I pushed him so hard that he fell out of his chair and landed on the floor. When he went down, he took his bowl of spaghetti with him. It splattered everywhere. Tomato sauce dripped from his overturned chair like blood.

"Emma! Stop it right now!" Mom yelled.

"Did you see what she did?" Jacob accused from where he was lying on the kitchen floor.

I could feel my face getting as red as the tomato sauce. "I'm not a tree hugger!" I blubbered, with big tears flowing down my face. "I'm just smart enough to care about the environment!"

"Jacob, you're not hurt. Get up and clean yourself up," Mom ordered. "And then go to your room so Emma and I can talk."

Jacob did as he was told, glaring at me the whole time. "Tree hugger!" he said one last time, loud enough for me to hear but too low for Mom to make it out.

"Emma, Jacob was wrong to tease you, but you were wrong to push him," Mom said when he was gone. "What's this all about?"

"I can't tell you," I shouted between sobs.

"Why not?"

"Grandma Hazel made me promise not to."

"Honey, who is Grandma Hazel? Your grandmothers are named Barbara and Natalie."

"Oh." I took a deep breath and looked at the floor.

"Come here." Mom pulled me onto her lap like I was a little girl and offered me a tissue.

"What's this all about?" she asked again as she consoled me.

"Well, it's just that I have a hard assignment to do, and I can't talk about it."

"Is it some school work you're supposed to do over your summer vacation? Should we talk to Mrs. Morgan about it?"

"No, it's not homework from her. That won't help."

"What will help?"

"I don't know. Nothing. It's just a hard assignment," I said.

"What makes it so hard?"

"A lot of things." Sir Charles, who can smell spilled food a mile away, had come into the kitchen as soon as Jacob's bowl hit the floor and licked up most of the spaghetti and some of the tomato sauce. Now he made a little whimper and licked my hand.

"It's complicated," I continued. "I want to do something, but I don't know how. And it's such a big project I don't know where to start."

"Ah." Mom nodded. "I've found when I have a big job to do, I often put it off, and then it becomes even bigger and harder in my head."

"Uh-huh."

"But you know what? I've also learned if I break the big job down into smaller steps and just concentrate on taking the first step and getting it started, before you know it, I'm doing it!"

"I'm not sure that will work for me," I said.

But Mom was on a roll. "Do you know what I always find hard to do? Wash the kitchen floor," she said. "I absolutely hate washing floors."

"You do?" I asked. "I didn't know that."

"Well, I hate it," Mom continued. "I like having clean floors, but I don't like to do the work to clean them. So every week when the dog and you kids track stuff onto the kitchen floor, I tell myself I'll just spend 15 minutes cleaning this floor, and then I'll stop to do something else. Sometimes I even set the timer for 15 minutes. Sometimes I crank the radio up high and play music while I work. Do you know what usually happens?"

"What?"

"Usually after I do the hard part of getting started, the 15 minutes go by quickly. And because I want a clean floor more than I want to stop, I keep going. It just seems easier to keep at it than to stop. Before you know it, the floors are clean until the next time you all get them dirty!"

Mom looked at me closely and continued. "It's rare when I have to set the timer for 15 more minutes. Once I get started, I just do it."

I thought about this for a bit. I wasn't sure it would work for me.

Mom stroked my hair. "My own mother used to say, 'A job begun is half done.' Do you know what that means?"

"Not really."

"It means often the hardest part of a job is tackling it. Once you quit putting it off and begin, it often isn't nearly as hard or as awful as you thought it would be, and before you know it you're well on the way to finishing it!"

Mom was such an optimist.

"Well, maybe I'll try that," I said, unconvinced.

"I think you'll find it's helpful," Mom said. "Of course there are some tasks you have to do research for, or undergo many years of training to accomplish," she added. "And some jobs require teamwork. I mean, being a doctor and doing brain surgery or something like that is much different than washing a floor. But everyone still gets to a point where they just have to try their best, go for it, and start."

I wanted to tell her the problem was I didn't know how to start, let alone complete the job, but I couldn't. I had sworn to Grandma Hazel and Santa to keep everything a secret. I didn't think she would believe I'd been to the North Pole anyway.

Mom was full of suggestions. "Setting a deadline can help too," she said.

"Another idea to consider is the divide-and-conquer method. Making a list of all the steps in a job and spreading out the work between additional people is another way to get things done," she added. "That's what we do with the chore chart on the whiteboard in the laundry room. Everyone has at least one job to do each week to help the house run smoothly."

"I know about that," I said. My job is filling and emptying the dishwasher. "But no one can do this job except me."

"Once you get started it won't be so bad, I promise," Mom assured me. "You can do it if you try! And remember, you can tell me anything. If you have a problem, I'm right here. I love you."

"Thanks, Mom," I said. I took a deep breath and hugged her around her neck. "I love you too."

"Now, let's put the lunch dishes in the dishwasher, and I'll start on this floor again." Mom sighed, but she gave me a quick kiss.

I slid off her lap and put the plates, silverware, and glasses into the dishwasher, closed the door, pressed the correct buttons, and then went to my room.

Mom had given me lots to think about. I'm not sure if I felt better, but it was good that I didn't tell my secrets.

My Secret Spot

The next day was Saturday.

I thought a lot about what Mom had said. I did have some help in all this. Mr. Strauss, the editor of "The North Pole Times," promised he would help, and he was an experienced journalist and editor. Hopefully he'd be able to fix my mistakes and make my book good enough. And Santa knew everyone — literally. He could probably help or get others to help too. Both he and Grandma Hazel have magical powers, so there was always that too.

In the afternoon I borrowed the timer from the kitchen. It's yellow, with black numbers on its dial. Hopefully Mom wouldn't miss it for a while.

I put the timer, one of my little notebooks, and a pen in my pockets and headed for my secret spot. Everybody knows I go there a lot so that's not the secret. The secret is once I'm there, no one can see me.

My secret spot is where two big branches come together in one of the two chestnut trees in our backyard. My spot is just low enough that I can climb up into it easily. It's just high enough that the tree's shiny green leaves hide me. No one can see me unless they know where to look.

It's up about 30 feet, I guess.

It's an excellent place to think.

Once I climbed up, I removed two brown chestnut tree burrs where I usually sit, being careful not to get stabbed by the bristles. They were both about the size of a small apple, but the chestnuts had already fallen out of them. I dropped them to the ground and made myself comfortable. When I looked up, I could see the bright blue sky with wisps of white clouds. I could smell the rich aroma of grass since Dad mowed the lawn last night.

A little brown wren watched me from a branch above me on the left, and it chirped to say "Hi!" I could also see a little brown bunny searching for clover in the lawn below me. A crow cawed from somewhere; I could hear him but couldn't see him. A caterpillar hunched along a big limb below me, and a daddy longlegs climbed up my left leg. I picked him off it and put him on a limb below me, where he continued his walk like he had somewhere important to be and was very late.

I thought about all the animals and insects that called this tree home, and how amazing it was. I wondered how old it was, and decided it was probably at least 100. I wondered who planted it 100 years ago. Trees are pretty incredible. No wonder Blitzen loves them so much.

I thought about how worried Blitzen is about global warming. I thought about the magic lichen and scraped a little green growth off the limb I was sitting on, near my right hand. I wondered how to make kids want to change their habits and save the Earth. I wished I had my notes, but they were flying in the wind somewhere near the North Pole.

I set the timer for 15 minutes and pulled out my little notebook and the pen. The pen was one of my favorites. It was plastic and in the form of a blue icicle. It made me think of Santa's Kingdom. I drew the outline of a pine tree at the top of the first page. A breeze cooled the air and whispered through the leaves.

How should I start?

It might be a good idea to start telling the story at the beginning. That was the night I met Grandma Hazel and got beamed up to a magical new world beyond the Northern Lights.

On a Roll

The timer went off, and I kept writing. I could barely get it down fast enough, as the words just tumbled onto the paper! It was as if my heart would burst if I couldn't get it all down.

I wrote for most of the rest of my summer vacation. The only time I took off was the week I went to church camp.

Although I didn't use the timer again, I did use my alarm clock. Writing seemed to go best in the morning, when it was quiet, before Jacob got up.

I often wrote from my secret spot in the chestnut tree. Sometimes I wrote at my desk in my bedroom, with Pansy curled up close by. On days when I wrote at least three pages, I gave myself a sparkly sticker on that date on the "Frozen" calendar in my bedroom. As the summer went on, more and more stickers dotted the calendar.

I still didn't know exactly what to say to convince kids to take conservation seriously, but I went on, hoping they'd get the idea somehow.

Maybe if I put all the reindeer's tips in the book, the kids could start by doing one or two, and then it would get easier as they went on. Maybe if we all just started doing one or two things better, we'd end up doing many things better. And maybe together we really could save Christmas and the Earth.

When my nerves got bad I made myself think about Mr. Strauss. He was an experienced editor, and he said he would help organize my manuscript and fix it. When I met him he seemed up to the task. He was a nice man. After all, he bought me a nice briefcase before he even met me.

I wrote almost every morning, and sometimes in the afternoons too. I wanted to tell someone about my trip to the North Pole so badly that the words just spilled out.

Without notes, I told most of the story from my memories. When I couldn't remember something, it would often come to me at night in my dreams.

I finally understood what Mom meant when she said I just needed to apply myself. I used to think, "Apply myself to what? I'm not glue." But she meant I had to work hard. And it was really hard work.

Mom noticed I was working hard on something, but she didn't confront me about it. The only thing she said was that I was more moody than a soap-opera character who had just discovered she'd been cut out of the family fortune.

I rolled my eyes and kept writing.

Finally, one day I decided the story was done. I still didn't know if it was good enough, but I didn't know how to make it any better either, and I was sick of trying and second-guessing myself. I put all the pages in a box and got it ready to mail.

I enclosed a letter to Grandma Hazel.

Dear Grandma Hazel,

I don't know if this is good enough to make kids change their bad habits. I don't know if enough kids will take it seriously and begin to conserve and recycle more. Even if we all work together, I don't know if it will be enough to save Christmas and the Earth.

All I know is that I did my best, and I finished something.

Love,
Emma

I sealed the box with very strong tape and got a mailing label from the desk in the kitchen without Mom seeing me. I addressed it to "Grandma Hazel, Gumdrop Ave., Santa's Kingdom, North Pole." I rode my bike to the post office, where I spent my allowance on stamps and sent it off.

Then I waited.

The End Is Just the Beginning

I waited a long time without hearing anything. I convinced myself that my package was in the "lost letters" bin at some post office somewhere. However, one night at precisely 7:57 p.m. as I had just finished my homework in my bedroom, I heard the faint sound of bells and Grandma Hazel appeared beside my desk.

I was so glad to see her! We exchanged a long hug.

"Emma, I loved your book!" she whispered.

"You did?" I asked, hoping she wasn't just being nice.

"I loved it," she confirmed. "So did Santa. He just tweaked a few things, and then we gave it to Bob Strauss to edit. He said he didn't want to change much, so that it was in wording that kids use. He said all he did was fix some grammatical things and spelling here and there, and then he tightened it up a bit."

"I didn't know it was loose," I said.

"It must be journalism talk," Grandma Hazel said.

"Now will we send it to an agent or a publisher?" I asked.

"Pfft." Grandma Hazel made a funny sound by pursing her lips and letting air go through her lower teeth. "As you know, the environment can't wait. Publishers have too many meetings and take a long time, so we took things into our own hands. It's important that the book is available for kids to read as soon as possible. And we think it's great!

"The cover art is done. The elves worked nonstop to translate the manuscript into all the human languages of the world. Santa ordered 'The North Pole Times' to suspend publication temporarily so the book could be printed in all the different editions needed for children around the world. It's on the press as we speak."

"It is?"

"Yes. And on Christmas morning every child will receive a copy of it delivered personally by Santa. And everyone who gets an e-reader for Christmas will automatically find a copy on it."

It was all so exciting!

"Our distribution system is even better than Amazon's," Grandma Hazel added with great pride.

"Here, I have an advance copy for you," she said as she thrust a book into my hands.

It was beautiful. There was a picture of Blitzen and me on the cover, with the Northern Lights above us. The title, "Emma and the Reindeer," was in big, swirly letters with my name in smaller swirly letters at the bottom. It was all so amazing that tears started flowing down my cheeks.

"It really happened!" I said. "I finished something, and I wrote a book! Maybe I do have gumption! And maybe kids will read it and save Christmas and the Earth!"

"We're all so proud of you. And of course each reindeer likes her chapter the best." Grandma Hazel chuckled.

"Do you think it will work? Do you think it will make children everywhere care enough to change their ways?"

"That's the billion-dollar question," Grandma Hazel said. She jumped up and kissed me on my forehead and then she was gone. It didn't surprise me that she disappeared because I know that's one of her traits, and I also know how much she hates goodbyes.

So that's where we stand. The ending of this story is up to you.

The Reindeer's Tips

Dasher: Turn off all electronic devices when you're not using them.

Dancer: If you haven't already done so, replace regular lightbulbs with LED lightbulbs. Compare the energy costs of new products and old products that need replacing. Often buying something new will save more energy and money than fixing an old product that isn't as energy conscious. Learn about wind power and windmills.

Prancer: Use less hot water. If you have a dishwasher, use it instead of hand-washing dishes, and let them air dry. Take shorter and cooler showers. Wash clothes in cold or warm water instead of hot water. Don't let the water run when you're brushing your teeth.

Vixen: Adjust your thermostat. Moving it down just 2 degrees in winter and up 2 degrees in summer will save energy. Programmable thermostats make that easy! Also learn as much as you can about solar energy, as it's the cleanest and most abundant renewable energy. There are now government programs that make solar panels for homes more affordable than in the past.

Comet: Recycle, recycle, recycle! Recycle products and household waste. Don't litter! Composting is great! Stop buying bottled water. Use reusable water bottles, filters, and tap water instead!

Cupid: Avoid products with a lot of packaging. It's essential to keep everything we can out of landfills. Write to companies to ask them to use biodegradable packaging. Also bring your own reusable bags to the grocery store.

Donna: Ask your parents to drive less, use energy-friendly cars when they do drive, and service them regularly. Slow down and speed up gradually. Walk, bike, carpool, or take mass transit more often. Keep tires inflated properly. Electric cars are the wave of the future. Lobby your government officials to tell them saving the environment needs to be a top priority.

Blitzen: Plant as many trees as possible. Take up gardening or buy local produce. Take responsibility for your actions where the environment is concerned. Don't wait for someone else to do it. You must make changes to save Christmas and the Earth. We must all work together. If we can save the environment, it will be the most important thing we will ever do.

About the Author

Emma Gallagher is a sixth-grade student in Mrs. Morgan's class. She lives in the Midwest in the United States with her parents, her brother, a dog named Sir Charles, and a cat named Pansy. She loves to read, and she's thinking about becoming a reporter or a writer when she grows up. "Emma and the Reindeer" is her debut novel, unless you count an unfinished manuscript in a box under her bed.

Emma would like to thank Santa, Grandma Hazel, all the reindeer, Isabella, Benny, and Mr. Strauss for their help. She'd also like to thank her mom for the productivity tips, and especially **you** for reading her book!

Emma's favorite author is Linda Mansfield, who also helped a bit. Linda is a reporter, editor, and public relations representative who lives in Indianapolis, Indiana, in the United States.

Linda is a long-time reporter for "Speed Sport News." She owns a motorsports PR firm, Restart Communications, LLC. She is also the part-time communications coordinator of North United Methodist Church in Indianapolis.

Like Emma, Linda is trying to stop procrastinating and become a better steward of the Earth.

Linda enjoys the challenge of fiction writing. It's a way for her to stretch her wings, because it's very different from the inverted pyramid of newswriting she usually uses in her work.

She wrote four books of fictional short stories for teenagers through senior citizens that you might like to check out. You can learn more about "Stories for the 12 Days of Christmas," "Twelve

Stories for Spring," "Twelve Stories for Summer," and "Twelve Stories for Fall" and sign up for her free readers' club on LindaMansfieldBooks.com. You can also follow her on Facebook (Linda Mansfield — Author) and Bluesky (@RestartLMAuthor). She is most active on Facebook. You can also email her at EmmaAndTheReindeer@gmail.com.

Both Emma and Linda would also like to thank the following people: Chadwick Gillenwater (aka Professor Watermelon) of the Indiana Writers Center (initial critique provider); Jessie Raymond (first-round editor); Carola Clark, Oliana Elmore, Lorna Johnson, Nena Ray, Wanda Clark Resler, Jeanita Schulten, Dick Slease, and Jennifer Tavitas (beta readers); Emily Nemchick (post-beta proofreader); critique providers Alexandra Weiss, Ashley Hearn, Kelly Barrales-Saylor, and Cheryl Klein through the Society of Children's Book Writers and Illustrators' webinars and other events; an unnamed critique writer through Book Pipeline; developmental editor Susan Korman, and our cover illustrator, Enkelejda (Lejda) Ramo.

Emma and Linda would love for you to leave a positive review at any of the online outlets that support reviews, like Amazon, Barnes and Noble, and Goodreads. Reviews help readers decide if they'd like to read a particular book. They help authors gain exposure and an audience, provide credibility with publishing professionals, and ultimately increase sales. Reviews do not have to be long, but they're very important to a book's success. Writing can be a solitary endeavor filled with many second thoughts and rejections, so a positive review tells authors that you connected with their writing and encourages them to persevere.

Linda Mansfield with Hope, a 4-year-old female reindeer owned by Silly Safaris, Inc. of Indianapolis, on Dec. 21, 2024. The location is The Shops at Perry Crossing, an open-air shopping center in Plainfield, Ind., which incidentally has a wonderful Barnes & Noble store! (Marti Humphrey photo; photo editing by Rich Barker of Barker Graphics)

Back cover photo: Aurora, Oct. 10, 2024, McCloud Nature Park, North Salem, Ind., photo by Linda Mansfield.

About the Cover Artist

Enkelejda (Lejda) Ramo's love for art began as a child and kept growing throughout her life. During her time in art school she immersed herself in various art forms, experimenting with different mediums and techniques. The enchanting landscapes and nostalgic streets of her hometown of Korca, Albania, fueled her creativity.

When she immigrated to the United States from Albania in 2000 her passion for art had to take a back seat, as the responsibilities of building a new life became her priority. The demands of adapting to a new culture and ensuring the well-being of her four children took precedence over the canvas and brushes.

However, her love for art never faded. As her children grew more independent she found the chance to reconnect with her artistic side. She said this journey of rediscovery has been truly magical, and with every brushstroke she is rekindling that vibrant artistic spirit within her.

Lejda is now based in Avon, Indiana, where she creates stunningly realistic, one-of-a-kind personal portraits and other compositions in many different formats. She chose pastel pencil on heavyweight pastel paper as her medium for the cover of "Emma and the Reindeer," which shows Emma with Blitzen.

For inquiries or questions about her custom drawings and paintings see her website at ArtByLejda.com; her Etsy store at ArtByLejda; follow her on Instagram (ArtByLejda), and email her at artbylejda@gmail.com.

Enkelejda (Lejda) Ramo

Everybody Loves 'Emma and the Reindeer'

Kids:

"A beautiful and creative way to introduce the subject of climate change and how to prevent it to children." — Paige Crawford, 12.

"I loved it!" — Oliana Elmore, 12

"It's a good book. It makes you want to do things to help the environment." — Mia, 11, last name withheld upon request

Parents/Grandparents:

"As a grandparent of two 12-year-old girls, I feel you did an excellent job of getting into the thoughts of a preteen. The book's subjects are well researched and have a fun flair. I very much enjoyed the mix of fantasy and reality, along with the ancestry elements." — Nadene Bruce, mother of four and grandmother of six

"I loved it! This book is magical, and it brought back so many wonderful memories of my childhood Christmases. I loved that the book was educational and addressed recycling and climate change, which are important to me too." — Barb Hoover, mother and grandmother

"I encourage all middle-grade students to read about Emma's magical journey to the North Pole. Emma is chosen to write a children's book to empower young readers to believe they can make a difference." — **Wanda Clark Resler**, mother of two, grandmother of eight, and great-grandmother of six

"'Emma' is a creative and engaging sleigh ride full of joy and struggle that children of many ages can both relate to and learn from. For experienced environmentalists and those just starting to contribute, 'Emma' will have you cheering for our girl, our planet, and the magic of Christmas alike." — **Jennifer Tavitas**, mother-to-be

Teachers:

"Well done! The words were beyond descriptive and truly painted a detailed picture of Santa's magical kingdom. Isabella was the star of the show for me. She sold the whole story. Tears pooled. I love that both fiction and fact were interlaced to bring awareness to such an important issue, as well as spark the magic of Christmas." — **Elizabeth Reed**, kindergarten teacher

"Un cuento de fantasia que nos encanta por el viaje de una niña a la tierra de Papá Noel donde entrevista los venados. Aprende mucho de las vidas de ellos y lo que todos nos toca hacer para guardar nuestra planeta." — **Jan Wheater-Cowen**, retired Spanish teacher

(Translation: "A fantasy story that we love because of a little girl's journey to Santa's land, where she interviews his reindeer. She learns a lot about their lives and what we all have to do to save our planet.")

Other People Who Are Fluent in Other Languages In Addition to English:

““Emma und die Rentiere” ist eine inspirierende Geschichte, die zeigt, dass wir alle individuell eine wichtige Rolle spielen, die Erde, die wir so lieben, zu beschützen. Ein schönes weihnachtliches Abenteuer für Kinder.” — **Carola Clark**, a native of Germany

(Translation: “Emma and the Reindeer” is an inspiring story showing that we all individually play an important role in protecting the Earth we love so much. A beautiful Christmas adventure for children.”)

Librarians:

“A wonderful Christmas read-aloud for the entire family. Especially fun for the middle-school reader who may enjoy holiday memories while learning about tasks to help Santa’s reindeer save the environment.” — **Ruth Diffenbaugh**, retired librarian for Fairfax County, Va.

“The young heroine learns about the effects of climate change from a very unlikely source! An entertaining and informative read. I highly recommend it.” — **Susan M. Wever**, retired library director

Authors:

“Linda Mansfield’s wonderful middle-grade novel, “Emma and the Reindeer,” is an absolute delight. Readers of all ages will fall in love with Emma Gallagher, Grandma Hazel, and the rest of the marvelous (and frequently magical) cast of charming, chummy Christmas characters. Brace yourself for an exhilarating, enchanting adventure to the North Pole to learn the secrets of Santa's workshop that they don't want you to know. Prepare to be moved, both emotionally and to action. Our environment needs all of us to act. With the aid of her new friends, Emma will share practical tips for what young readers can do to pitch in. I cannot recommend "Emma and the Reindeer" highly enough." — **Rob Kent,** author of "Banneker Bones and the Giant Robot Bees" and host of the popular podcast and website MiddleGradeNinja.com

"Linda's talents are magical. Her charming descriptions evoke a truly wonderful visual of Santa's North Pole village that clearly has been a secret until now. Her clever personalities for each reindeer are so much fun and weave the story together like perfect Christmas mittens. A true delight, Emma's adventure will fuel imagination and passion for every reader." —**Lee Anne Patterson,** author of "The Trouble With Howard;" see TheTroubleWith-Howard.com

"Emma and the Reindeer" is an enchanting novel that reads like a fantasy while confronting global warming. It will enthrall, entertain, and educate. It is a brilliant book that addresses global warming without confrontation, and provides insightful information. It's a keen way to introduce STEM education, and a must-read for children interested in ecology." — **Brad G. Philbrick,** founder of Brad G. Philbrick & Co., a pharmacist, grant proposal writer, copywriter, and author of "Musings of a Most Observant Man: The House Always Wins"

"I really believe that young people today don't have enough wonder and imagination in their lives. I loved the idea of disappearing into Christmasland in the middle of a non-Christmas calendar.

"I think writers need to do more to take young people behind the curtain of make believe and ignite their imaginations, awe, and wonder. There isn't enough imagination, awe, and wonder in a video game! I think Emma started down that road for us.

"I loved the reindeer personalities. I really loved Dancer! A reindeer in a purple scarf dancing the samba brings a mental image that can't help but summon imagination and laughter.

"She may have been aiming at 8-to-12-year-old readers, but their parents and grandparents might find this appealing as well! I think we're entering a cultural period when adventure, imagination, and escape might be just what many people need." — **Bill Wood**, author of the young adult novel "STEM Stories: When Racing Goes to School and Grows Up"

Celebrities:

"Please read Emma's excellent book and follow my reindeer's tips. Together we can make small changes that will be a big help in our fight against climate change. They will also ensure that I can continue to visit the good boys and girls around the world each Christmas Eve!" — **Kris Kringle**; saint, toymaker, gift giver, world traveler, reindeer rancher, and keeper of the "Naughty and Nice List."